# GRANNY'S GOT A GUN

## A SECRET AGENT GRANNY MYSTERY BOOK 1

### HARPER LIN

This is a work of fiction. Names, characters, organizations, places, events, and incidents are either products of the author's imagination or are used fictitiously.

GRANNY'S GOT A GUN

Copyright © 2017 by Harper Lin.

ISBN-13: 978-1987859454

www.harperlin.com

## ONE

**I** was at the weekly meeting of the Cheerville Active Readers' Society, the closest thing to pass for entertainment in this sleepy little New England town. I found myself living here after I retired from the CIA.

I'm Barbara Gold. Age: 70. Height: five feet, five inches. Eyes: blue. Hair: gray. Weight: none of your business. Specialties: undercover surveillance, small arms, chemical weapons, Middle East and Latin American politics. Current status: retired widow and grandmother.

Addendum to current status: bored out of my skull.

Like my retirement, forced down my throat by

the government three years before, the book selection for that month was not going down well.

*Endless Beach* was a classic romance novel from 1912 that had recently been reissued as part of a major publisher's "Forgotten Female Authors" series. It should have remained forgotten.

An obvious Jane Austen knockoff, written in an era when a wee bit more physical contact was permitted (Kissing! Gasp!) but lingering Victorian morals ensured a tepid read, it came off as old fashioned even in a reading group in which the youngest member was sixty-five, reading glasses were universal, and wrinkles had long stopped being a source of worry. Despite the story being a snore, it had managed to enthrall most members of the reading group, although for different reasons.

The seven members sat around the coffee table in Lucien and Gretchen Rogers's living room, a circle of gray hair, wrinkles, and persistent aches and pains. Gretchen's prize-winning lemon cake sat on the table, with only one piece left.

I stared at the cake with annoyance. As usual, Gretchen had used some delicious icing to write her favorite line from that week's reading assignment. This week it said: *Like the sand on the beach, our love is renewed with every crashing wave.* That corny line, which didn't make all that much sense, epitomized both the novel and Gretchen. A bit corny, a bit nonsensical, so it came as no surprise that it stuck out to her, a beach-obsessed hopeless romantic.

She and her husband, Lucien, had both turned sixty-five that year, and while Lucien had settled into placid retirement, Gretchen was going through something of a late midlife crisis or a really late puberty. She dreamed of being whisked away by a handsome stranger to some gorgeous beach somewhere. Their house was adorned with photos of the Bahamas, the Seychelles, the Maldives, and other exotic locales, all taken by someone else. As far as I could tell, the couple had never been farther than Maine.

Gretchen, as usual, had cut the cake into eight pieces. Why she did this, I could never figure out, because that last slice of cake always ended up sitting on the plate for the rest of the meeting. No one ever took it. Not that anyone was watching their figures too closely at this late stage of life; it was simply that taking a second piece would be rude, and rudeness was something that just wasn't done in Cheerville. You wouldn't want to irritate anyone, after all.

But that extra piece irritated me almost more than I could bear. I hadn't made it through a Cold

War and several hot ones by being sloppy and wasteful, and leaving an extra piece no one had the gumption to eat was the epitome of sloppy and wasteful.

So I frowned at it again. The icing spelling out the words "crashing wave," the only words left, seemed to mock me. In a few minutes, Lucien would clear the table and toss out the spare piece.

I had received the piece that read "renewed," but Cheerville was doing anything but renewing me. In fact, I had developed a deep fear of fossilizing.

I wished the reading group had continued with *Behind Open Curtains*, this month's first choice until everyone cracked the cover. It had been billed as "romantica," a subgenre everyone thought was some new spin on romance. Nobody had bothered to Google it. If we had, we would have found out that it was an amalgamation of "romance" and "erotica." Pearl, another member of our group, who at ninety-six years of age should have seen it all by now, had nearly had a coronary at the phrase "throbbing man root."

"Throbbing" was a word often seen in *Behind Open Curtains*, as was "pulsating," "yearning," "moaning," and "clenching." There were even a few yelps and ululations. Just who the heck ululates in bed, anyhow? And there was so much fire symbolism in *Behind Open Curtains* that those curtains must have been made of asbestos.

I fully intended to finish reading that one. I needed to get to the bottom of this ululation business. Had I been doing it wrong all these years?

"Barbara?"

The voice sounded insistent, as if it had spoken my name before.

I looked up to see everyone staring at me. How long had they been saying my name? How long had I been thinking about that stupid slice of cake and strange bedroom noises? I was losing my edge, getting soft. When I still worked for the CIA, nothing ever went unnoticed around me.

"Yes?" I answered.

"What do you think about Victor's betrayal? How could he leave his wife after twenty years?" asked Pauline, a plump woman of seventy-two with thick cat's-eye glasses. The ache in Pauline's voice told me that she'd felt that same betrayal in her own life, meaning the question was loaded and couldn't be answered the way I would have liked.

Evon, Pauline's best friend and a spinster ex-schoolteacher, reached over and pointed to my book. She had a bad habit of doing that, as if everyone was a slow pupil.

"The scene is on page seventy-one," she said. "What do you think about it?"

Judging by the smiles on the faces of my fellow book club members, everyone loved *Endless Beach*. Even Lucien and Charles, the two men in our group, had enjoyed it, or at least pretended to. I didn't. I especially didn't like Marcella, the lead character. Marcella's husband, Victor, had walked out on her after twenty years. This "betrayal" happened early in the novel and was the catalyst for Marcella coming out of her shell to find new and lasting love. The problem was that Victor was painted as the bad guy, a selfish cad, while the author put Marcella on a pedestal as the paragon of faithful wifehood.

But Marcella had no sense of adventure, no passion, no initiative. It wasn't until Victor left for his own adventures in Paris that Marcella could even conceive of the idea of abandoning the comfort of her hometown and think of her dreams as anything more than just fantasies.

If I had been married to someone like that, I would have left in the first year, not stuck around for twenty. Not that my James had ever been boring. A bit too turned on by demolition operations, perhaps, but never boring. However, for this group, that was the wrong answer.

I turned to the page, put on my reading glasses, and tried to hedge my bets.

"Well, Marcella had loved him unconditionally for twenty years, so to leave her just because he thinks he can be a painter in Paris is, um..."

"Maybe he was gay. That's why they called it 'Gay Paree,' isn't it?"

This was from Pearl, who sat slumped in an easy chair like a Gothic ruin.

"It's Barbara's turn, Pearl," Gretchen told her, almost shouting so that Pearl's ninety-six-year-old ears could hear her. Gretchen always hosted and had decided that this meant she was in charge.

I tried to think of a way to finish my sentence that would be a reasonable compromise between how I actually felt and something these small-town conservative senior citizens could accept.

But what could I say, that I had ditched my college boyfriend of three years right after graduation, the boyfriend who had gotten down on one knee and proposed marriage, because I'd preferred to join the CIA and hunt terrorists and narcotraffickers? The worst of it all was that I had actually said yes to him and then changed my mind and never regretted that, heartbreak or no heartbreak. Painting in Paris seemed tame compared to what I had done.

"He's a quitter. A selfish jerk. Marriage is forever, and you have to stick with it through thick and thin."

That came from Lucien Rogers, Gretchen's husband, mumbled through the last bite of his slice of lemon cake. His response actually made me wince, and I hoped no one noticed.

Lucien was a bit dim, but nice—too nice, really. I could stand up and put him in a chokehold until he passed out, and he'd probably thank me, assuming I had done it out of the best intentions. The fantasy of doing just that briefly flickered through my mind. I had to give him credit, though. His being such a sweetheart did come in handy. As much as I hated to admit it, there were plenty of things I could no longer do, and more and more got added to the list every year.

When a tree had fallen and blocked my driveway after a snowstorm in my first week in Cheerville, Lucien had swung into action, chainsaw in hand. I knew how to use one as well, if not better, than Lucien, but I'd have had to cut that tree into pieces not much bigger than sawdust in order to move them without hurting my back.

Lucien didn't even know me at the time. He had simply been driving past my house and saw the fallen tree. His chainsaw happened to be in his trunk. I got the sneaking suspicion that, once the snowstorm had finished, he had driven around the neighborhood looking for people who needed help. After he invited me to the reading group and I got to know him better, that suspicion turned into a near certainty.

This guy was remarkably fit for his age. He wasn't hard on the eyes, either, so nobody objected to his patrolling the neighborhood offering to help out. Nobody female, anyway.

Lucien, obviously feeling pleased with himself by closing the conversation with such a sparkling insight into *Endless Beach*, started to clear the table, collecting plates and forks and the platter with the lone piece of lemon cake with its mournful phrase, "crashing wave," on it before disappearing into the kitchen. I watched it go, knowing it was destined to be eaten by some undeserving rat in the town landfill.

That was a shame, because Gretchen's cake really was delicious.

The chatter continued as the other members of the club freely spoke their minds on the tragedy of giving up on something you've been building for twenty years. Everyone agreed that Victor had acted like a cad.

"The author should have written a sequel in which Victor fails as a painter and drinks himself to death with absinthe," Charles proclaimed, emphasizing his point by thumping his cane on the carpet. Charles was the local funeral director. For some reason, no one objected to his presence. While I had been dancing with death all of my professional career, most people liked keeping anything associated with the Grim Reaper at arm's length.

I sighed and leaned back in my chair. They'd skipped my turn, but I didn't mind at all because it let me off the hook. It was the end of another faintly amusing but really quite dull meeting of the Cheerville Active Readers' Society. I had grown tired of Cheerville so quickly—tired of the people, tired of living alone, tired of the prosperous, straight-laced dreariness of it all.

I changed that prognosis immediately when Lucien fell dead in the kitchen.

# TWO

Lucien didn't go out with a bang but with a thud—the unmistakable thud of a body hitting the floor. I had heard that thud many times before. In fact, I'd been responsible for that thud on a number of occasions. That thud, like so many identical thuds, was followed by a profound silence.

"Lucien?" his wife, Gretchen, called. More silence. "Lucien!"

Knowing something was seriously amiss, the Cheerville Active Readers' Society sprang into action. Actually, "springing" into action wasn't an option. Our springing days were over. Trying to rush into the kitchen would have most likely ended with all of us joining Lucien on the floor.

In reality, it was less of a spring and more of a grumbling, pained struggle to lift ourselves up, grab canes and walkers, and make our way carefully to the kitchen door. Pauline grabbed her walker. Charles grabbed his cane. I said a silent word of thanks that I still didn't need either. Pearl stayed put because staying put was what she did best. Evon stayed behind with her, either out of concern for the group's oldest member or out of fear of what might greet her in the kitchen.

Together, the rest of the Cheerville Active Readers' Society carefully worked their way into the kitchen. At a certain age, you've seen your fair share of dead bodies. We were all at that age. I'd been at that age by thirty. The senior citizens around me had seen countless friends and family members laid peacefully in a wooden box. However, most were accustomed to seeing those familiar faces with hair combed, eyes shut, and makeup applied to hide graying skin. They saw their loved ones as they were best remembered—about to meet the good Lord dressed in their Sunday best.

That was not how Lucien looked. Instead, he looked much more like the bodies I'm used to.

Lucien lay flat out on the kitchen floor, a pool of blood slowly spreading from his head from where his skull had cracked against the linoleum. The dishes were scraped clean and neatly stacked in the sink, with the glasses set in a neat row on the counter next to it, ready for washing. Lucien had been an eager helper to the last.

Gretchen covered her mouth with her hand to hold in a shriek. Pauline's hand wasn't fast enough, and a scream, quite high pitched for such a large woman, jabbed my ears like a volley of pistol shots at a gunnery range when you've forgotten to put on your earmuffs. Charles grunted, meaning to speak but unable to form words. Despite dealing in death on a daily basis, his stomach hadn't quite hardened, and the shock of seeing one of his friends stretched out on the floor must have hit him hard. I covered my mouth and looked appalled because that's what they expected. No need to let them know that I've seen scenes like this before. In fact, I've seen much, much worse.

Even so, seeing someone I knew, and someone five years younger than me at that, suddenly dead was not how I wanted to spend my Sunday afternoon.

It was Pearl's voice, calling in the warbling, scratchy ninety-six-year-old throat, that got the group moving again.

"What's happening in there? Was that Pauline screamin'? Did Lucien wet his pants or something?"

As a matter of fact, he had. That's what happens when you die: you lose control of your bodily functions. Not very glamorous. Hollywood tends to skip that little detail.

Pauline shuffled out of the kitchen to deal with Pearl, obviously more than happy to get out of sight of the gruesome scene. Gretchen rushed to her fallen husband, the tears flowing down her wrinkled cheeks. She said his name what seemed like a hundred times, but all the *"Luciens!"* in the world wouldn't bring him back. Charles approached, checked Lucien for a pulse that he did not find, and put a calming hand on Gretchen's back.

I hovered near the doorway, wondering about Pearl's question. Just what did happen in here? At Lucien's age, your chest can tighten up on you at any moment. Two heartbeats can be one away from your last at any given moment. That was the obvious explanation.

Lucien took good care of himself. He exercised regularly. I knew this because I'd enjoyed the view of him on his morning jog on many occasions. He ate well. I knew this, too, because Gretchen loved to cook and loved even more to brag about the health-conscious meals she prepared every day.

But heart attacks sometimes don't care about how well you've lived. Sometimes they're happy to take the healthy down into the dirt right alongside the fast food–gorging couch potatoes.

Sometimes, however, the most obvious explanation is not the correct one. I have never been one for obvious explanations.

I approached. Everything in the kitchen seemed in order. There was nothing on the counter other than a few kitchen appliances. I didn't see any bloody knives or a rat scurrying away. I didn't see any bees that might have stung him and caused an allergic reaction. The stove was electric, not gas. There were no threats in this kitchen.

Stepping around Gretchen, who still knelt, her face pressed against her dead husband's shoulder as the undertaker tried to comfort her, I took a look at the body.

Lucien's tongue and lips were swollen and stiff, not a common symptom of heart attack—more akin to an allergic food reaction. Lucien, however, had no food allergies. Again, I knew this because Gretchen loved to talk about their meals at every opportunity.

His pupils were dilated. Most importantly, I noticed a buildup of thick saliva around his mouth.

Whatever was inside him, his body didn't want it there and was building up saliva in order to empty his stomach's contents. It was his stomach that was his problem, not his heart. The fall might have been what actually killed him or might have prompted a heart attack, but he was well on his way toward death before taking the plunge.

Lucien had been poisoned.

This hadn't been a slow process, either. Most toxins take hours to have any effect. Some take days. Whatever had killed Lucien had acted fast and must have been administered within the last hour or so—or to put it plainly, sometime during the weekly meeting of the Cheerville Active Readers' Society. Someone in this house was a murderer.

A little chill ran down my spine, not of fear—I can take care of myself—but of excitement. I know it sounds cruel, but this was the most exciting thing that had happened to me since my retirement. A murder right in front of me, and me personally acquainted with the murderer!

But who was it?

Lucien Rogers was a good man, a good-natured soul. The British would call him a good egg. He deserved better than to be quickly cooling on a linoleum floor. The house with those linoleum floors wasn't his only home; the entire neighborhood was his home. But while Lucien was a charming fellow, he was actually a prime candidate to become a murder victim.

He was a pillar of the community in the truest sense of the term, always willing to lend a hand (or a chainsaw) to anyone in need. He was easy to find and was even easier on the eyes. That was the only reason I could immediately come up with that someone would want to hurt Lucien. He certainly rubbed a few husbands the wrong way because he was the standard against which they were all measured. If they were above sixty, that is. The older women of Cheerville changed their posture when he came around, standing up straighter. Their voices rose, higher and sweeter. A bit of lust twinkled in their eyes. I can admit that I've felt it myself. And through it all, Lucien just gave the ladies that winning smile, helped shovel snow from their driveways or change tires on their cars, and as far as I knew, never let his popularity go to his head. Just as he had said earlier in the meeting, "marriage is forever." In fact, those were his last words.

Helpful. Handsome. Humble. A dangerous combination bound to attract envy and spite.

Charles's voice snapped me out of my thoughts. He was on the phone with 9-1-1, informing them of the death, identifying himself to the woman on the phone, who apparently knew him, and giving the details. After he hung up, he gently led Gretchen back into the living room.

I followed, wiping a tear from my eye. That tear reassured me. I had seen a lot of death in my time, and had caused a fair amount of it, too, but I had never become any more hardened than what the job absolutely demanded.

Once out in the living room, I hardened again. One of these five senior citizens was a murderer, and I was the woman who could discover the culprit.

Gretchen? The odds suggested that it was her. Most of the time when a married person gets bumped off, it's the spouse. The motive was usually one of three things: money, abuse, or an affair. Lucien didn't have much money and shared it all with Gretchen anyway, plus he wasn't the abusing kind. People have surprised me before in that department, but that was well beyond the realm of possibility. An affair? Lucien didn't seem the sort of person to cheat. From what I'd heard, he had refused many offers. In fact, he had refused someone in this very room.

Pauline had been entranced with Lucien even more than was usual among the gray-haired belles of Cheerville. Perhaps that was because her husband had left her many years ago for a younger woman. That's why she took the plotline of *Endless Beach* so personally. At seventy-two, more than a little over-weight, and relying on a walker, she hadn't exactly been Lucien's most fetching offer, but when she had opened up her heart to him a few months back, the guy let her down easy. So easy, in fact, that she stayed in the reading group and everyone got along.

At least on the surface. Could Pauline be angry and hurt enough to kill her autumn love? Or could Gretchen suspect the two had been having an affair and decided to bump Lucien off? Or maybe I had it all wrong and there really *was* an affair? I didn't know enough to say. Once again, the grinding polite-ness of Cheerville meant that I didn't know much about that whole mess.

Then there was Evon, also seventy-two and a childhood friend of Pauline. She hadn't come into the kitchen when we heard Lucien fall. She was a hypochondriac, so that reaction was understandable, but perhaps she avoided confronting the body because she feared her reaction would betray her guilt. But why would she want to kill Lucien? As revenge for breaking her friend Pauline's heart? Or maybe she had a thing for him, too.

She was the person in the group I knew the least, since most of my conversation with her involved enduring long monologues about her imaginary physical complaints. Calling her a hypochondriac was an insult to the mental stability of your average hypochondriac. And that made me wonder if she could kill someone even if she wanted to. On the other hand, when you fear death so much, you tend to think about it all the time, and that can twist one's mind.

What about Charles? The sixty-eight-year-old mortician still worked every day, partly to keep his mind off his own grief. His wife, Laura, had died of a horribly aggressive thyroid cancer the year before. I had never met her but heard she had been quite the party gal. Could there have been some history between her and Lucien? If there was ever a man more devoted to his wife than Charles, I haven't met him. He still talks about her as though she was still alive. He would go to his own grave with his heart completely hers. But what if he discovered something that changed his perspective?

Also, it was no secret that Charles's business was suffering. It was not something he liked to talk about, but he didn't need to. The town did the talking for him. A new funeral home had opened up in a nearby town and had taken much of his business. It was a chain and could offer lower rates. I hadn't realized that funeral-home businesses could be franchises. "Do you want fries with your coffin?"

Funeral directors are known to be a bit morbid, and there are stories of them boosting business through rather nasty means. A struggling funeral director in Georgia found himself in a fix when his cremation oven broke and he didn't have the money to repair it. Apparently, cremation ovens cost a pretty penny, and he was already badly in debt. The bodies kept coming in. Instead of taking a loan to fix the oven, he decided to dump thirty bodies in a swampy marsh on his land and give grieving families concrete dust instead of the remains of their loved ones. It's heinous, but that doesn't mean it doesn't happen. But was Charles capable of not just heartless deception, but cold-blooded murder? Would he poison a close friend just to sell a coffin?

If that was the case, why Lucien? There were many Cheerville families much better off than the Rogerses. If you were going to knock someone off, wouldn't you want to take out someone who will spring for a king's casket as opposed to the bargain box that Gretchen was sure to buy?

Least likely was Pearl, who at ninety-six was by far the oldest and feeblest in the group. I couldn't think of a motive, but that didn't mean a motive didn't exist. She had a sick sense of humor, and she was the only one whose eyes weren't wet. Perhaps she had seen so many friends die that she had come to accept death as a regular occurrence. Or perhaps she didn't mind that Lucien had keeled over. I'd have to check that out.

I'd have to check them all out.

I looked at Gretchen, who had her face buried in her hands, shoulders shaking as Charles tried and failed to comfort her. Pearl sat in her armchair looking grim, her snappy and off-color sense of humor silent for once. I looked at Evon, the hypochondriac who constantly checked WebMD to see what she might have come down with this time, now staring at the kitchen doorway as if the Angel of Death himself stood there leering back at her. And I looked at Pauline, who sat there with a stunned, lost look.

Which one?

# THREE

I drove through the tree-lined streets of Cheerville, passing well-manicured lawns and whitewashed Colonial-style houses while trying to sort out my thoughts. I had kept quiet when the EMTs had taken Lucien's body away. The county coroner would notice the telltale signs of poisoning and prompt an investigation. The police would do their best to find the culprit, and perhaps they would succeed, but I couldn't be sure of that.

I had a better chance to do that myself. First off, people wouldn't be on their guard when I talked with them. I also wouldn't be buried under a big caseload like every single homicide detective I'd ever met, and I'd met a lot.

A part of me felt guilty. I'd had too much training

and had lived too long not to know myself inside and out. I knew I wanted to investigate this case because my life as a grandmother in Cheerville had begun to grind me down. This was the most exciting thing to happen to me since getting shot at in Cairo, and that had been almost five years ago. So I had to ask myself —was I interfering in police business only because I wanted some thrill in my life?

No, I was right to keep my mouth shut. The murderer would be someone in the readers' group, and I had an excuse to see all of them anytime I wanted and pump them for information without their realizing my true motive. That, combined with my professional background made me the most qual-ified person to investigate the murder.

But how much time did I have before the police started knocking on doors and putting everyone on guard? That depended on the coroner's caseload. He had to see the body, make a preliminary diagnosis that the death was suspicious, perform an autopsy, send some blood and tissue samples to the lab, and get the results back.

Of course, the police might get involved right after the coroner did the autopsy. The coroner's initial suspicions would be raised, but the lab results would be the clincher. The cops wouldn't want to wait for the lab results, which might take a week or more, so they might start on the coroner's recommendation right after the autopsy. It was a Sunday, though, so the whole process probably wouldn't start until tomorrow. So I had what—two days? Three at the very most.

I had to act fast. The problem was, I had to let everyone cool down for a bit. The whole readers' group was stunned and would need some time to sort themselves out.

Gretchen would be talking with various officials. Charles had stayed with her, being accustomed to death and handling the bereaved loved ones of the recently dead. The others had headed home to deal with their shock and sorrow however they needed to. I would have to put off starting my questioning until tonight at the absolute earliest.

So I did what I always did when I was on a mission and had to endure some mandatory downtime—I put the situation on the back burner of my mind and focused on something else. It was an old trick that had served me well. The subconscious made connections while the conscious did other things. Even science supported my practice. Numerous studies had found that "sleeping on it" actually improved creativity and problem solving.

I headed over to my son's house.

Frederick, his wife, Alicia, and their thirteen-year-old son, Martin, lived in a pleasant New England–style home with a leafy yard at the end of a quiet cul-de-sac. In fact, most people in Cheerville lived like this. The town was embarrassingly prosperous and homogeneous. I'd rather live in Cairo or Medellín any day.

But my only son and my only grandson lived here, and after my husband James died, I couldn't think of anywhere else I'd rather be.

I pulled into the driveway, narrowly avoiding my grandson's bike dumped half on the lawn and half on the pavement, and cut the engine.

As I hauled the bike onto the grass, my back gave me a nasty twinge. I went to the front door and rang the bell. Frederick had given me keys and told me to come over anytime, but I didn't like barging in. I valued my privacy, and I wasn't about to intrude on someone else's, not even someone's whose diapers I had once changed.

After a moment, I heard Frederick's heavy footsteps. What forty years ago had been the *pitter-patter* of little feet had now become the *thud thud thud* of a grown man rapidly entering middle age. There was the click of a lock and the slide of a bolt. Frederick had put that bolt in himself, to "protect his family," he said. I smiled. Why did people invest in bolts when the average American front door was so flimsy a single good kick would knock it in?

Not that that sort of thing happened in Cheerville. Briefly, I wondered when the last murder had occurred in this upper-middle-class bubble of white picket fences and gourmet cheese shops.

"Mom! Nice to see you. Come on in."

My son greeted me with unaffected joy. I smiled, flush with gratitude. Considering all the times my dear departed husband and I had left him for weeks at a time with relatives while we were on assignment during his childhood, he had every right to feel sullen and distant, and yet he had never shown us an ounce of disapproval. He had never known what all that "government work" really was, and yet he had accepted it and loved us both. It had been a no-brainer to move here after James passed away.

"Make yourself at home. I'm just preparing some dinner. We're having microwave pizza. Want some?"

"Um, no thanks. Did Alicia get called away again?"

My daughter-in-law was a particle physicist, doing something I didn't understand with the CERN reactor beneath the border of France and

Switzerland. Some big research project kept her flying over there at a moment's notice. It was my greatest fear that they'd move to Europe for the sake of her job.

"Yeah. She's headed down to JFK now," my son said.

A loud beep came from the kitchen.

"Looks like your *haute cuisine* masterpiece is ready to wow the culinary world," I said, following him down the front hall. "When is the Food Channel signing you up for a show?"

"Two words—frozen meatballs," Frederick shot back with a smile.

An old joke. Bad cooking ran in the family. Once when Frederick was eleven, I'd served spaghetti and meatballs, with the meatballs coming frozen from the supermarket. I thought I'd heated them up enough, until my son bit into one and chipped a tooth on the frozen core. Luckily, it was a baby tooth that he lost the next year anyway. He still remembered, though. He also remembered it hadn't been my worst attempt at cooking.

Passing into the living room, I saw my grandson, Martin, slumped on the couch, his feet propped on the coffee table as he played *Call of Duty* on the Xbox. The thirteen-year-old was slaughtering a host of enemy targets with the ruthless efficiency of a KGB or Mossad operative. I knew. Oh, I knew.

"Hi, Martin!" I said cheerily as I sat down beside him.

The only response was a tank exploding. The graphics were beautiful, but tanks didn't sound like that when they exploded. My grandson stared at the screen through bangs that desperately needed trimming. His unruly blond hair seemed to go in all directions at once. I used to love to tousle that hair. Now, I didn't dare.

"Martin, say hello to your grandmother!" Frederick called from the kitchen.

"Hello," he mumbled.

"Say hello to your grandmother!" Frederick called again.

"I DID!"

More enemy targets got taken out in a spray of gore.

"How was school?" I asked.

"Good."

"What did you study this week?"

"Things."

"What kind of things?"

"Stuff."

"I was always pretty good at Things class. I had a bit of trouble with the Stuff section, though."

Martin gave me a look like I was the most boring old fart in the world then went back to staring at the screen.

I winced. When he had been a toddler, I had been "Nan Nan!" When he had been an adorable little boy flying into me with the force of a meteor, I had been "Grandma!!!" Now I was "Martin, say hello to your grandmother."

"Dinner's ready," Frederick called from the kitchen.

Martin paused the game in mid-massacre and thumped off to the kitchen, leaving me alone on the couch. Letting out a sigh, I looked at the screen. Martin was using an M16, although I knew from all the times I had watched this game that he had a bunch of weapons and an unlimited supply of ammo. I'd have loved to tell him how I'd used all of those weapons in combat and that you had to conserve your ammunition, since nobody could carry an unlimited supply. A few stories about my missions would certainly get his attention. All that was classified, however. I could tell him, but then I'd have to kill him.

With another sigh, I extricated myself from the

sofa and headed into the kitchen. Frederick and Martin sat hunched over the small breakfast table, shoveling cheap microwave pizza into their mouths. The dining room was never used when Alicia went away because Frederick was too lazy to set it, and Martin wasn't exactly the kind of kid who did chores.

I sat down in the spare seat and watched them for a moment.

"How's the real estate business going?" I asked my son.

"Still pretty flat thanks to the downturn," he said, taking another bite of radioactive pepperoni. "Got some good leads, though."

Ever the optimist. I could gauge the ups and downs of Frederick's business by how often I was called to babysit. Most prospective buyers scheduled house visits after work and school hours, and with Alicia away so much, that left me taking care of Martin. Not that he really needed taking care of, but when he was playing video games, he was as much of a zombie as the ones he killed in some of his games. The house could fall down around him while he was defeating the level boss, and he'd never know it.

I used to love babysitting. Now, I mostly sat in a corner reading while things blew up on television.

"How was your reading group?" Fredrick asked.

I had been dreading that question.

"Well, not so good. Lucien died. It was quite sudden."

Frederick's jaw dropped. Even Martin looked up from his plate.

"What happened?"

I shrugged, feeling the sadness wash over me. Funny how it hadn't really hit until I told someone who didn't know Lucien.

"He collapsed. It looked like a heart attack."

*Looked like.*

The tears started to come, not so much for Lucien, but for James. My late husband had been just as handsome, just as helpful, and way more intelligent. Even better, he had been mine.

Martin got up and gave me a big hug.

"Sorry you lost your friend, Grandma."

I buried my face in his unruly golden locks and hugged him back. He squeezed me harder. He was getting tomato sauce on my blouse, but I didn't mind at all.

# FOUR

Later that evening, I had the perfect excuse to start my investigation. Evon called me in a tizzy, saying she was suffering heart palpitations. She knew I was trained in first aid—one of the few details I give out about my training because it's good for everyone to know who can help in an emergency—and Evon wanted me to come over right away.

Of course I did, but not because I was worried over her health. She did enough of that for the both of us. No, Evon wasn't having heart palpitations any more than she had come down with thyroid cancer after Charles's wife died. That was just her hypochondria kicking in. On some level she knew that, too, because she hadn't called the doctor. Every physician, nurse, emergency medical technician, and veterinarian in Cheerville had told her the same thing—you are remarkably healthy for your age, and you have no dangerous conditions or illnesses. That wasn't what she wanted to hear, and they weren't giving her what she really wanted—sympathy. I could provide that, plus a visit would give me a chance to grill her.

Evon lived alone in a cute little cottage not far from my son's house. As I knocked on the front door, I caught a whiff of disinfectant. The doorknob gleamed brightly in the setting sun, and I could see telltale streaks that showed it had been wiped recently. I bent over and gave it a sniff. Yes, disinfectant.

"Barbara, is that you?" Evon's voice came from behind the door.

I stood up abruptly, my back giving another angry twinge. The peephole was dark. She'd seen that I had been bent over. Would she wonder why?

The door opened, and the smell of disinfectant became stronger.

That wasn't unusual. Evon feared germs the way the CIA used to fear communists. They were invisible, sneaky, deadly, and everywhere.

Evon clutched her chest and looked at me sorrowfully.

"Thank the Good Lord you made it in time. I feel like I'm dying!"

*At our age, aren't we all?* I thought. I kept that to myself. Speaking it aloud might push her over the edge. The Cheerville Active Readers' Society didn't need *two* murderers.

"So what's the problem?" I asked as I followed her into the living room. Everything looked scrupulously clean, as usual. An aspirin bottle and a large bottle of mineral water sat open on the coffee table. Evon slumped down on the couch, and I took out my first aid kit, which I always kept in my car.

"Let me have a listen," I said.

I had a stethoscope in the kit. I wasn't really qualified to use it, but I didn't use it for listening to heartbeats anyway. A good stethoscope works wonders for listening at doors and walls.

I warmed up the stethoscope as well as I could by rubbing it against my palm—the stethoscope my doctor had used during my last checkup was so frigid that it nearly gave me a heart attack of my own—and listened to the faint *thump thump thump* of Evon's seventy-two-year-old heart.

Timing her heartbeat with my watch, I found it a

bit elevated but suspected that with a chronic worrier like her, it was always elevated. I didn't hear anything else amiss.

That was not what Evon wanted to hear, of course. She wanted to be the center of attention and worry. I had to make more of a show of this.

"I'll check out a few other things," I said. "Let me listen to your lungs."

Evon removed her blouse like a professional. No, not *that* kind of professional. I mean a professional patient. I suspected she loved to have her lungs listened to. Who knows how many times she caught pneumonia and bronchitis in a single week? And then there was that new strain of tuberculosis that was resistant to all medication. She loved that one.

"Take a deep, slow breath," I told her.

I needn't have bothered—she was already doing it like she had done it a million times before for a million exasperated doctors.

Her lungs sounded fine.

"I feel weak and dizzy," she said.

"Maybe you need to eat something."

She shook her head. "I can't eat a bite, not after what happened."

Poor Evon. That part, at least, I understood. I

decided to give her the full treatment and took her blood pressure, too.

"I have terrible blood pressure, very high. Actually, life threatening."

Actually, she did have high blood pressure, hardly surprising given her nature. But life threatening? No.

"Well, it does seem your blood pressure is a tad higher than normal—"

"I knew it!" she said, falling back on the couch with a satisfied groan.

"But your heart rate and lungs are fine."

"Nonsense! I'm at death's door. My whole body feels off kilter."

"You're just distraught over what happened to Lucien. We all are. I'm sure my blood pressure is up, too."

Evon's eyes widened. "You want me to check yours?"

"I'm sure I'm fine."

The last thing I wanted was to become her sister in misery.

"What do you think killed him?" she asked, worry stamped on her face. "Could it be that new form of tuberculosis going around? It's mutated and immune to all known medicines."

I knew that was coming. I was tempted to reply that it might be Ebola, but that would be cruel. Hilarious, but cruel.

"Lucien wasn't coughing. If he'd had tuberculosis, he would have been coughing."

"I heard him cough once or twice," Evon said defensively.

"He'd have to cough a lot more than that. Lucien didn't die of tuberculosis. He died of a heart attack."

I said this last bit to catch her off guard.

"Just like I'm going to die of a heart attack! What am I to do? I take aspirin every day like you're supposed to and get regular checkups, but the doctors are all quacks and say there's nothing wrong with me. I know there is, Barbara. Maybe I have a heart murmur."

"You don't have a heart murmur."

Actually, I wasn't qualified to say that, but since none of her army of physicians had detected one, I felt I was on safe ground.

"Do you want some mineral water?" she offered. "It's good for purifying the system."

"I'm fine," I replied, resisting the urge to edge away.

I wasn't going to eat or drink anything from any

member of the reading group until I cracked this case.

She poured herself a tall glass and gulped it down.

"Poor Lucien," she murmured.

I studied her. She had a look of relief on her face. Why? Because Lucien hadn't died of something she could catch? Or because I had pretended to be fooled about the murder?

I needed to dig deeper.

"Yes, poor Lucien. Everybody loved him," I said with unaffected grief.

"Well, I wouldn't go that far," Evon replied.

*Now we're getting somewhere.*

"What do you mean?" I said in mock surprise.

"Well, you know some husbands were a bit jealous. All the men our age are wasting away, catching the most horrible things because they let their immune systems decay by drinking beer and sitting on the sofa all day. I don't even like to be around men our age. I'll catch something for sure. But not Lucien. He was the picture of health. I always envied him that. That's why it's so worrying that he just up and died. It came out of nowhere."

I thought for a moment. Jealous husbands? I'd noted that before, and it was the most likely motive, but we didn't have any jealous husbands in our group, unless Charles could have discovered something between Lucien and his late wife. That seemed a bit thin but worth following up on.

"I never heard of men resenting Lucien," I said, faking surprise. Playing the new woman in town could come in handy. I'd been in Cheerville for a year, but it was the kind of small town where you're considered a newcomer for a lot longer than that.

"Oh yes, they grumble and grouse all the time just because he is healthier than they are, or at least he was."

"Charles too? I've never heard him say anything!" I said, pretending to be scandalized.

"He was one of the only ones who didn't," Evon replied, putting her forefinger and middle finger on her wrist to check her pulse. "He always respected Lucien, and you know how Charles doted on Laura, especially after she fell sick. I'm glad he's taking care of the funeral arrangements and not that new place. I suspect he'll be burying me soon. I've already arranged for a lovely casket and floral arrangement. I'll look better than I have in decades."

This last was said with a sigh and a swoon. I found it interesting that Charles had already cornered the market on Lucien's corpse.

Evon looked at me suddenly. "Would you mind hosting the next reading club meeting?"

I blinked in surprise. "Um, I suppose I could. Why?"

Immediately, I cursed myself. I had already half said yes to something when I didn't know what it was all about. It would bring a poisoner into my home. Or was that Evon's intention?

"It's just that if there really is something floating in the air in Gretchen's home, I don't want us all to catch it."

"There's nothing floating in the air," I replied, realizing that my words came out sounding like a scoffing doctor. She'd heard that attitude a million times before.

No invisible microbes had killed Lucien. One of his friends had. So who did it? Could it have been this trembling wreck in front of me? I found it hard to believe that she could summon the courage to poison anyone. Her hypochondria wasn't a front. Pauline had complained that Evon had been like this since she was a kid. When everyone got the chickenpox in fifth grade, Evon had been convinced it was smallpox and had taken it upon herself to call the Centers for Disease Control. Why they listened to a ten-year-old girl was anyone's guess, but an entire isolation unit had shown up at her house. Evon's parents had been mortified.

"So will you host the meeting?" she asked again.

"Well, I don't know if there will be a meeting next week considering what happened."

"No, I suppose not, but we'll start meeting again soon enough, and I don't want to risk going back into that house."

"Well, you have a lovely home, why not—"

"Out of the question! It's hard enough keeping this place clean without having a lot of people coming and going. Oh, I don't mean to offend, Barbara. You take care of yourself. But there's Charles handling all those bodies, and Pearl at death's door, and Pauline has never taken care of herself, and even you could catch something from that grandson of yours. Kids these days are so filthy. I don't know how I ever survived being a school-teacher. I'm sure it undermined my health."

"I'm surprised you can bear going to PTA meetings."

Evon was still quite involved in the school district. Like me, she resented the inactivity of retirement.

"I take a good, thorough shower every time I come home from one. Volunteering at the library is even worse. Those books. Ugh! Who knows where they've been? That's not the worst, though. You know the kids are catching viruses from computers now?"

"Evon, I know you retired from teaching quite some time ago, but surely you know the difference between a computer virus and an actual virus."

"I'm not talking about computer viruses! Just think of those keyboards and the mouse! All those grubby fingers touching them. Do you know how many germs are in the average booger?"

"Don't tell me. I don't want to know. I'll think about hosting. Perhaps one of the other members will volunteer."

It didn't look like I was going to get any further that evening, so I bade Evon good-bye, leaving her with her complexes and simplexes and fatal conditions. It hadn't been as useful a visit as I had hoped, but it was a start.

# FIVE

The next morning, I woke bright and early as usual. I'd gotten into the habit when I was in the field doing CIA work and never got out of it. People fantasized that when they retired, they would sleep until noon every day. I knew that would never happen with me. I'm just not that kind of person. There was too much life to be lived and not enough time in which to live it.

People also fantasized about having a peaceful, quiet time for their remaining years. After all I've been through, I had been kind of hoping for that too. Now it looked like that wasn't going to happen. I had a murder investigation fall into my lap, and the murderer was someone close to me. I had to proceed with caution. If they thought I was snooping around, they might try to poison me, too.

I practically leapt out of bed. "Practically," I say, because leaping isn't something I do as well as I once did. But I did haul myself out of the sack with a fair amount of enthusiasm. A peaceful retirement wasn't my style. The year-long snoozefest I'd endured since moving to Cheerville was over. I finally had something interesting in my life.

The question was: what to do next? I needed to talk to Gretchen as soon as possible. Being the victim's spouse, she was the prime suspect. I couldn't think of any real reason why she would want to kill Lucien, but I was playing the odds based on decades' worth of homicide statistics. Spouses kill each other; it's a sad fact.

I checked the clock. 6:10 a.m. Too early to call. Gretchen was a senior citizen and had strange sleep patterns like most people our age, and she probably hadn't slept a wink anyway whether she was guilty or innocent, but calling at six in the morning was rude even by septuagenarian standards. I ate my breakfast and showered with impatience. I hated inactivity.

I didn't have to hate it for long. My phone rang at 6:40.

I picked it up.

"Hello, Barbara? This is Pearl."

I held the phone away from my head. Pearl's hearing hadn't weathered the past ninety-six years too well, and she always shouted.

"Hello, Pearl. How are you?"

"Better than Lucien. Have you talked with Gretchen yet?"

"No, why?"

"She wants me to go over there. Can you drive me?"

Bingo.

I was at Pearl's house within minutes. She already stood at the door waiting for me. Like all people I've met in their nineties, Pearl wanted her way all the time, right this instant. I suppose that's natural when you're four years shy of a century. Procrastination is a bad idea for anybody; for someone like her, it's the same thing as saying you're not going to do something at all.

Unlike Charles, who used a cane, and Pauline with her walker, Pearl didn't need any assistance except someone to lean on. That someone was Fatima, a Nicaraguan nurse who lived in Pearl's spare room. Fatima was a smiling, professional woman in her thirties who dressed in an immaculate white nurse's uniform and spoke good but heavily-accented English.

"Now Ms. Pearl, I could have driven you myself," she was saying as she led her patient down the two steps from her front porch to the walkway.

"Nonsense!" Pearl barked. "Do they even have driver's licenses in Mexico?"

"I'm from Nicaragua, Ms. Pearl, and yes, they do."

"Probably get them out of cereal boxes. Do you have cereal boxes in El Salvador?" Pearl grumbled.

"Nicaragua. We go to a government office just like you do. And I have an American driver's license too."

"You do? How could you read the exam?"

Fatima didn't respond to that. Well, actually she did, by muttering some very coarse and unladylike phrases under her breath in Spanish. Pearl, being nearly deaf, didn't hear a thing.

I, being fluent in Spanish thanks to fighting communist guerrillas in Fatima's home country, understood every word.

I tried to hide my blushing. I didn't want Fatima or anyone else to have any hints about my past. Besides, listening to Fatima cussing out her patient was one of my favorite parts of the day.

Fatima helped Pearl into my car, and I thanked her. Pearl didn't.

"You should really be kinder to Fatima," I said as we pulled away. "She's always very nice to you."

"Oh, she's all right. Makes a good cup of tea and remembers my medicine. But you can't trust these Ecuadorians to drive. Did you hear about that fifteen-car pileup they had down there? It was all over the news."

"Fatima is from Nicaragua."

"Yes, and they had a fifteen-car pileup down there. It was all over the news."

I rolled my eyes and changed the subject.

"So how is Gretchen holding up?"

"How should I know? That's why we're going over there to check."

I raised my eyebrow. It was barely past seven, and there were few cars on the road. Monday-morning rush hour, or what passed for rush hour in Cheerville, was still an hour away.

"You didn't talk to her this morning?" I asked.

"No."

"I thought you said she wanted you to come over."

"Of course she wants me to come over. Her husband just croaked."

Oh dear. We were going to show up uninvited in the early morning at the house of a grieving widow. Well, at least we'd catch her off guard. That wasn't such a bad idea, and I could always blame Pearl for the mix-up. Everyone in town was accustomed to Pearl's pushiness.

We passed through Cheerville's downtown. While the town was small, it had a decent little shopping district in the center that served the town and the surrounding villages and countryside. A large, triangular village green edged with old oak trees took up the center. To one side stood a splendid old Colonial church that General Washington supposedly had prayed in as he took a break from one of his marches in the War of Independence. It was a fine structure of whitewashed wood with a tall steeple and one of the best preserved in the state. That brought in some tourists, who poked around the church and the eighteenth-century graveyard next to it before stopping off at the little one-room schoolhouse on the opposite side of the village green. All the local schoolkids took fieldtrips there to learn how their ancestors had been taught. Martin had proclaimed it "boring." Next to it stood a Colonial-era courthouse that now served as the home of the Cheerville Historical Society.

The south side of the green was taken up by a long row of shops, all in cute little Colonial-style buildings. Some of the buildings were actually old, but most were modern imitations, just like the majority of the houses in Cheerville. The residents all wanted to pretend they lived in George Washington's day, although they kept their cell phones and flat-screen TVs, of course. There's even a recreation of a Revolutionary War battle every year with Redcoats and Minutemen and a big booming cannon. That actually got Martin away from his Xbox for a couple of hours.

The businesses were what you'd expect for a chocolate-box commuter and tourist town. A string of antique shops face the village green, plus a couple of restaurants, gourmet cheese and wine shops, a café, a pet shop, and a few fashion boutiques. The more utilitarian businesses such as the supermarket, gas station, and a bar with a bit of a bad reputation, were all tucked out of sight behind the commuter train station on the other side of town.

We stopped at downtown Cheerville's one light, which had just turned red in our honor. Pearl peered out the window at the graveyard.

"You think they'll plant him in there?" she asked.

"I don't think anyone has been buried there for more than a hundred years."

"So where will he go? Potter's Field?"

"I'm sure Gretchen has a nice plot somewhere."

"She'll probably just have him burned up and toss the ashes somewhere and good riddance."

"Pearl!" I shouted, scandalized. Gretchen was one of my main murder suspects, but that was no excuse for rudeness.

"Oh, she won't miss him at all. She'll be living it up in the Bahamas in no time."

"Why do you say that?" I asked, intrigued. Pearl could be pushy and impatient and downright rude, but she'd lived long enough to have a clear view of people's character.

"You know how she's always pining to go off to some tropical paradise. Just look at that art she has on her walls! And she's roped Pauline into helping her set up an aquarium. Like Pauline knows a barracuda from a hole in the ground! I'll bet you dollars to donuts that the day after Lucien is planted in the ground or his ashes are blowing in the wind like in that hippy song, she'll be on a flight to some island somewhere."

As the light changed and we pulled away from Cheerville town center and into a residential neighborhood, I considered that. Gretchen did always talk about how she wanted to travel, and she did fantasize about unspoiled beaches and tropical sunsets. Even the choice of this month's reading material, *Endless Beach*, was her idea of a mental getaway.

Her husband, Lucien, on the other hand, had been perfectly content to putter around Cheerville helping little old ladies who swooned at the mere sight of him. Being stuck with a husband who garnered that much attention while not being able to live one's dreams must have rankled. But was that motive enough for murder?

I found it hard to believe. Gretchen and Lucien seemed to get along just fine. I'd never heard her complain about him. In fact, I'd never heard her complain about all the ladies eyeing her husband. Pauline had fallen for Lucien, acting like a schoolgirl with a crush and being so foolish as to tell him. Lucien had been nice about it, told her he wasn't interested, and everyone managed to stay friends.

If Gretchen was so enraged as to actually kill her husband, would she be setting up an aquarium with one of his suitors?

Truth be told, none of the members of the Cheerville Active Readers' Society seemed like poisoners to me, and yet one of them had to be.

"Throat lozenge?" Pearl asked, offering me a little box of candied medicine.

"Um, no, thank you," I replied, tensing.

Even Pearl could be a murderer.

We pulled up at Gretchen's house to see her garage door open. Gretchen was just visible behind the family car, putting a garbage bag into the big plastic container. She jumped a little as my tires crunched on the gravel driveway.

I pulled in behind her car, and she gave a little wave.

Two things struck me as odd—her throwing away trash at this hour and her jumping as we came up.

First, trash collection wasn't until just before dawn the next day, so there was no need to throw the garbage out now, especially since the bag didn't appear full. Second, why had she jumped at our sudden appearance?

Devil's advocate (or perhaps poisoner's advocate): Perhaps the trash contained something stinky she didn't want to keep in the house. Perhaps she was startled because of a sudden noise on her driveway when she wasn't expecting visitors.

A little more investigation would see what was right and what wasn't.

"Hello, Barbara," Gretchen said as I got out of

the car. Her eyes were bloodshot and rimmed in black. It was obvious she hadn't gotten any sleep. Grief or guilt? Hard to say. I remember not getting any sleep the first time I ever killed someone, and that had been a drug smuggler firing his AK-47 at me. Poisoning your husband of forty years would likely have a similar effect.

Of course, losing your husband without having murdered him would make you lose a lot of sleep, too. I knew all about that. After James passed, I didn't get a good night's sleep for a long, long time.

As soon as the thought crossed my mind, tears welled up in my eyes.

I hurried over to embrace Gretchen. I didn't know if I was comforting a murderer or not, but I knew I was comforting myself. After a long hug, I released her.

"How are you holding up, Gretchen?" I asked, wiping my cheeks.

Her cheeks were wet too.

"Well, he's with the good Lord now."

"Sorry for coming over unannounced. Pearl led me to believe she'd spoken with you."

"That's all right."

"We're all so terribly sorry about Lucien. He was a good man."

I studied Gretchen's face for her reaction to this statement but saw nothing but grief.

"I just don't know why it was so sudden," she replied. "He was so healthy. I know one shouldn't count the years at our age, but I thought we'd have fifteen, twenty more. I don't know how this could happen."

I did, or at least I had an inkling.

"Any word from the medical examiner?"

Gretchen shook her head.

"Charles is taking care of all that. He's been a rock. I suppose we'll hear later today."

Her words had a distant, stunned quality to them. It made me lean more toward "innocent woman in mourning" than "first-time poisoner shocked at her own ability to kill." I checked that line of thought. I needed to be objective.

"Is anyone going to help me out of the car?" Pearl squawked. She was trying to get out of the car herself, gripping the doorframe with her weak hands and tugging against the increasingly strong force of Earth's gravity. I'd been feeling it more in recent years myself. I hurried over. Well, I hurried over as much as Earth's ever-increasing gravity allowed. I used to be light on my feet. Now, I was simply grateful to stay on my feet.

I helped Pearl up, and together the three of us went through the garage to the open door that I knew led to the laundry room and, beyond it, the kitchen. I glanced at the garbage bin as I passed. I would need to take a look in there.

As we went through the kitchen, all three of us stared for a moment at the spot next to the sink where Lucien had fallen dead. There was nothing to show that murder had struck there. It was just a simple linoleum floor, freshly mopped.

We moved into the living room. Gretchen sank into the couch with an exhausted air. I helped ease Pearl into her usual armchair. I took the same chair I had sat in the day before in order to get myself into the feel of that situation. In one of the other chairs or on that couch, a murderer had sat through all of yesterday's meeting, waiting for Lucien to die. Less than twenty-four hours ago, Lucien had been alive and making worn-out old hearts beat a little faster, their ragged pulses get a little stronger. Now he was lying in the county morgue.

There was an awkward silence, as there always was in these situations. I had known plenty of death in the field and plenty of death as friends and family aged, but I had never yet figured out what to say. Because there really wasn't anything to say.

The silence did give me time to think, though.

The poison had most likely been administered in the refreshments, either the lemon cake or the lemonade. I thought back to how they had been served, imagining the room as it had been the afternoon before. I had deliberately taken the same seat as the previous day to help with that.

Gretchen had prepared both the cake and the lemonade. She was the star chef of the family. I couldn't recall Lucien ever cooking anything. Gretchen had come in and served the lemonade first, pouring it into each glass from a large pitcher. Obviously, the poison hadn't been in the pitcher, but a few drops could have been in the bottom of one of the glasses. They were bright-green tumblers that would have hid a few drops from view. Plus, many poisons were clear liquids, and thus, even if someone noticed, they would assume it to be water from when Gretchen had washed them. She could have given the poisoned cup to Lucien.

But wait, that wasn't correct. Thinking back, I clearly remembered that she had poured all the glasses and immediately gone back to fetch the cake. Everyone had taken their own glasses. Of course, they were set on a tray and everyone more or less took the one closest to them, but that was a risky proposition. If the poison went to the wrong person, she would have run the risk for nothing and killed a friend. Plus, she wouldn't be able to poison Lucien later without causing a great deal of suspicion.

So it had to have been in the cake. I focused, trying to summon up Gretchen's movements after returning with the cake. I remembered cringing at the quote she'd written on it with icing: *Like the sand on the beach, our love is renewed with every crashing wave.* Everyone had made the usual appreciative noises about the cake, I as much as the rest of them. Gretchen's cake was to die for.

Ahem.

So had she handed out the pieces, or had she set them on the table and let people take them? I really couldn't remember. I think I glanced back at my book and then started talking with Pauline. Or was it Pearl?

I thought for a while longer. Nope, it was gone. I had no idea how each person had ended up with their particular slice of cake.

It's incredible what small details can become crucially important later. I had been trained to understand this, had kept it at the forefront of my thoughts over many long years in tight situations. I can't tell you the number of times a sharp memory and an eye for detail had saved James and me.

But at seventy years of age, eating lemon cake in a gray-haired reading club in a dull town, I had forgotten that important lesson.

"Would you like something to eat? Tea and biscuits, perhaps?" Gretchen asked.

My heart turned to ice. Was she going to poison us?

"I'm fine, thanks," I was quick to respond. "I just had breakfast."

"That would be lovely. I'm starved," Pearl said.

I stared at Pearl in horror. What could I say to stop this?

Then reason and logic kicked in. If Gretchen was the murderer, she wouldn't poison us. That would cause too much suspicion, and, presumably, she had no motive. I couldn't even be sure she was the culprit.

Even so, I still couldn't help a sense of panic as Gretchen got up and moved into the kitchen.

"Let me help you," I offered, rising from my chair.

"No need," Gretchen said.

"I don't mind," I replied as I followed her. I wanted to see how she would react.

"Oh, if you must," Gretchen said. "I just feel I need to keep busy."

I followed her into the kitchen. She opened up a cabinet to get some tea bags and a tin of biscuits. I did a quick survey of the cupboard's contents before she closed it. Nope, no big bottle with a skull and crossbones on it saying "Deadly Poison: Guaranteed to off your hubby or your money back!"

This case wasn't making it easy for me.

I helped her brew the tea and set out cookies, feeling like I was conspiring with her to murder Pearl. Once we were done, we returned to find Pearl still ensconced in her armchair as usual.

Gretchen offered her some cookies, and the reading club's oldest member took a couple and started munching away with a contented air.

"You sure you don't want anything?" Gretchen asked.

"No, I'm fine, thank you," I said, trying to keep any traces of fear out of my voice as I gave a sidelong glance at Pearl. She seemed as healthy as ever, which wasn't saying much. She hadn't keeled over, anyway.

I turned back to Gretchen. "So, what happened? Did Lucien have heart trouble?"

Gretchen gave a sad little shrug. "I don't know. I

didn't think so. He had regular checkups, and the doctor said he was fine."

"It's his age," Pearl barked, a few crumbs sticking to her wrinkled lips. "Any of us can drop dead at any moment."

Gretchen went pale. I shot Pearl a nasty look that she didn't notice. At her age, people were in their own little worlds, and you either had to accept that or not spend time with them.

"May I use the restroom?" I asked, as much out of embarrassment as an excuse for snooping.

"Of course," Gretchen replied without hesitation.

I headed down the hall. The bathroom was at the far end, past the master bedroom and a spare room that doubled as a study. I glanced into both. The master bedroom looked the same as I remembered. The spare room now had a large aquarium against one wall. It wasn't filled with water yet, but otherwise, it appeared ready. Colored rocks filled the bottom couple of inches, along with a model of a sunken pirate ship. A pump was hitched to one of the glass walls. A few plastic containers stood on a small table next to it.

Glancing down the hall back toward the living room to make sure no one was looking, I entered the room and made a beeline for those containers. One was fish food, and the other two were for cleaning the tank. I put on my reading glasses and read the warning labels. While the labels said they should be kept out of reach of children, a quick survey of the contents yielded nothing that could have killed Lucien so quickly, if at all. Plus both were nearly full, obviously having been used only once to clean the new tank in preparation for it being filled with water.

Even if Lucien or someone else had put the small missing amounts of cleaner into his stomach instead of the tank, he would have only had a bad tummy ache. These aquarium supplies were not the murder weapons.

I set the containers back exactly as I had found them and continued to the bathroom. Closing and locking the door behind me, I did some more snooping.

Their medicine cabinet was almost devoid of medicine. Besides some aspirin and cough syrup, there was only a small eyedropper of glaucoma medication. The prescription label was made out to Gretchen Rogers. I hadn't known she suffered from glaucoma. A quick read of the warning label and contents showed that this could be chugged by the pint and not cause death.

I rummaged through the other cabinets and found nothing. Of course, there were household cleaning supplies that could kill, but they had an immediate corrosive effect on the mouth and throat. Lucien couldn't have sat through an entire meeting judging fictional characters for their lack of moral fiber if he had ingested some of that stuff.

Putting my hands on my hips, I gave the bathroom a frown. I was stumped.

I flushed the toilet and washed my hands, even though I didn't need to. Details like this were important in a cover story.

I returned to the living room just as Pearl proclaimed, "Well, at least you can take that trip to the Bahamas now."

Gretchen's eyes went wide, and she grew even paler than she had been when I'd retreated from the room. I couldn't help but notice, however, that her gaze briefly flicked to a photo of a beach of pure-white sand and turquoise water that hung above the mantelpiece.

Just then, my phone rang. The screen told me it was my son, Frederick. My heart did a little flip-flop. I had my chance to look in Gretchen's garbage.

I answered it.

"Hello, Mom?" my son's voice came over the line. Wait, phones didn't work on lines anymore. Funny how language takes so long to catch up with reality.

"Hello?" I said, and then louder, "Hello?"

"Yes, Mom, it's me."

"Hold on, the signal isn't very good on this darn thing. Let me go outside."

"But Mom, I can hear you just—"

"What? Just one second."

I made an apologetic shrug. Gretchen gave me a tired nod, and I walked out the front door, which was closer than the side door, so I had to use it so as to not arouse suspicion.

I'd already noticed that the blinds were down. She wouldn't see me as I crossed her front lawn.

As fast as my legs could carry me, which wasn't very fast at all, I headed for the garage.

"Hello, Mom? Can you hear me better now?"

"Yes, just fine," I replied as I entered the garage.

"I have a client who wants to look at a house this evening at six. Could you watch Martin for an hour or so?"

I paused. Time was ticking on my investigation. However, I couldn't think of a way to say no.

"All right. It will be just an hour or two, right? Things are still topsy turvy with Gretchen and everyone."

"I know. I'm sorry. But you know how Martin is. I can't leave him alone."

True enough. Thieves could come in and steal everything and set the house on fire, and as long as they didn't touch the TV or Xbox, the child wouldn't even notice.

"I'll be there at six. Bye," I said, hanging up.

Taking a furtive look around, I opened the bin, pulled out the garbage bag, and opened it.

SIX

An hour later, I dropped Pearl off with her nurse, who greeted me with her usual patient smile. I'm afraid I didn't smile back. I felt thoroughly confused.

The garbage bag had contained some burnt toast and a broken, uncooked egg. Gretchen, in her grief, had obviously made a mess of her breakfast. That explained why she had taken out a half-filled garbage bag. No one wants an egg rotting in their kitchen trash can.

The remainder of the trash included some junk mail, some paper towels that had been used to clean up the egg, and the remnants of our snack from the previous day's meeting. There was a heap of squeezed lemon halves, used paper napkins, and some excess batter, and frosting.

In other words, nothing that pointed a finger at Gretchen or anyone else.

And yet, something niggled at the back of my mind, something that told me that garbage bag and its contents weren't quite right. I couldn't put my finger on it. The shock of the previous day's events and the emotions brought up by my associating Lucien's death with James's kept me from thinking straight.

So I did what I always did to clear my head—I went to the firing range.

Yes, at seventy I was still going to the firing range. Nothing gets that old blood pumping better than squeezing off a few rounds. Of course, Cheerville didn't have a firing range, but there was one off the highway a few miles outside of town, tucked behind a gun shop.

The gun shop's giant billboard advertised "Guns, Guns & More Guns (and ammo too!)" beneath a huge .357 Magnum that poked out of the billboard to threaten the commuters. The billboard was a local landmark, and it had taken me a few months of going there before I discovered that "Guns, Guns & More

Guns (and ammo too!)" was actually the shop's name.

It certainly delivered. It had one of the most impressive stocks of firearms I'd seen outside of Pakistan. Everything legal could be purchased there, from the latest AR-15s to fine reproduction flintlock muskets. They had all the accessories, too, from camouflage outfits to telescopic sights. A big American flag hung over the door right beside a Colonial "Don't Tread on Me" flag with an angry serpent warning anyone against taking the customers' liberty.

I strolled in, carrying my 9mm automatic pistol in a locked carrying case as required by state law. I always followed the law unless I thought I or someone else was in danger, at which point the law became irrelevant and I did what needed to be done, like not telling the cops that Lucien had been murdered. While it might seem hypocritical to flout the law that I had sworn to uphold and protect, I was a former CIA operative, not a former Girl Scout leader. I didn't live in the same world as most people.

That became blatantly obvious every time I walked through the door of Guns, Guns & More Guns (and ammo too!). The store was one big room the size of a supermarket, with racks of guns and aisles of other equipment. The shelving was all fairly low, and anyone coming through the door was in full view of the other customers.

All those customers immediately turned and stared at the gray-haired grandmother toting a gun case.

All of them were men, every single one of them.

I gave them my sweetest grandma smile and strolled over to the front counter, feeling their eyes on me. It happened every time I came here, and I had to admit I enjoyed it. It was the most male attention I ever got these days.

Karl Nordenson, the owner, smiled at me from behind the counter.

"Hey, Mrs. Gold! Here for some shooting?"

Karl had long since gotten used to me. His customers had not.

"Yes, please. And a fifty-round box of 9mm."

"Coming right up."

A few minutes later, I stood in the firing bay of Guns, Guns & More Guns (and ammo too!)'s outdoor firing range. There was another firing range in the basement, but the weather was so nice today that I wanted to be outside. The sun was shining, the birds were singing from the tops of the nearby trees, and it was a perfect day to put some holes in some targets.

I put on my ear protection (my hearing is one of the few senses I still have at a hundred percent), set my pistol on the shelf in front of the firing bay, and studied the man-sized target set at fifty meters. Heads poked out of nearby fire bays, looking at me with curious stares or ill-concealed smirks. Those smirks got wider when I put on my reading glasses.

In one of the inevitable thefts of old age, I had become a bit far-sighted in recent years, and now I couldn't clearly see the sights on my pistol even when I held it at arm's length. I thought I heard a snicker from one of the guys. Actually, it couldn't have been a snicker if I heard it through the ear protection. It must have been a full-bellied guffaw.

I focused. Time to get rid of those smirks and make the guffawer guffaw from the other side of his guffaw hole.

In rapid succession, I placed all eight rounds in a tight cluster in the target's chest.

Your average Sunday shooter would have trouble putting four out of eight rounds anywhere on the target at that range, let alone in the kill zone of the central chest. A trained soldier would be expected to make six out of eight rounds on the target, with at least one or two in the central chest.

I'd put all of them there.

Soon I had a whole crowd around me, all asking the same question: "How did you do that?"

"Ex-army," I replied with a smug smile. That was close enough to the truth that it didn't feel like a lie.

Surreptitiously, I rubbed my wrists. The recoil on even a light pistol like this one had begun to hurt in recent years. I wouldn't even try to fire an M16 these days.

Ah, my dear departed husband just loved to see me toting one of those!

"There's something about women with automatic weapons," James always used to say with a sigh.

There was something else he always said too: "You're still going to be kicking butt when you're a grandmother."

I intended to.

I was going to solve this murder and make his angel give me a thumbs-up.

And then it struck me. I knew what had been missing from the garbage bag.

The eighth piece of lemon cake.

No one ever ate the eighth piece. There were seven of us in the Cheerville Active Readers' Society. Gretchen always sliced the cake into eight pieces. Helpful as usual, Lucien always cleared up the cups and plates. But it turned out the Good Samaritan had had another motive: clearing up the coffee table got him alone in the kitchen, where he could scarf the last piece of cake.

Did Gretchen know of this secret habit? Had she deliberately poisoned the spare piece, knowing that Lucien would eat it? She had cut the cake, and she'd doled out the pieces. With the cake conveniently written on, it would be easy enough to add the poison to a particular letter on the icing and leave that part as the leftover piece. It would sit there throughout the entire meeting like a time bomb, only to be set off when Lucien took it into the kitchen and ate it out of sight of the others.

It was perfect—she murdered him when she decorated the cake, but he only died when he was out of sight and she was still sitting in the living room acting all innocent.

I smiled to myself as I checked that my gun was out of bullets, put the safety back on, and placed it in its lockbox.

Okay, I had taken care of the who, so that left me with only two questions—how and why.

Wait, no, I still had the "who" question.

Because I had no proof that Gretchen was the one who had poisoned the icing, assuming it really was the icing that was poisoned. Someone else could have known of Lucien's secret cake fetish, and someone else could have planned the murder. It was entirely possible that the poison had been placed on the spare piece *after* the other seven pieces had been handed out. The spare piece sat on the coffee table amid all of us—that was what had always annoyed me about it—and people reached across it to pass each other books or to get more lemonade or another paper napkin.

It wouldn't take much sleight of hand to place a few drops of poison on it. All of us wore reading glasses, even Lucien. At many points in the meeting, all of us would be looking at the book of the month. All those tired eyes took a moment to look up and focus on the distance. Even if one of us noticed a fellow reading group member reach across the table and looked up to see what he or she was doing, by the time our eyes focused, the poison could have been dropped on the cake, the container for the poison palmed or tucked into a sleeve, and the murderer could have continued reaching across for a napkin or more lemonade.

I thought back to the meeting. Had I seen anyone reach across the table after the cake had been served? I couldn't recall, since my mind hadn't known that would be a significant detail. Even if I could remember with crystal-clear accuracy, I was willing to bet that I would have seen all of the reading group reach across the table at one point or another. Nervous little Evon, for example, always fluttered about, helping people with their books. Pauline tended to overuse the napkins and reached for extras throughout the meeting. Pearl made grand gestures as she shouted her opinions. Charles often helped get things from the table for Pearl.

So I hadn't proven anything. But I did know one thing I needed to do, and that was to get that garbage bag. If the poison was really in the icing and not dropped on afterward, that would be some pretty damning evidence against Gretchen. I had to get that garbage bag after it was placed on the curb in the evening and before the trash collectors picked it up in the wee hours of the morning. That should be easy enough for someone who had infiltrated Soviet military bases.

Of course, I had been half my present age and had had a well-trained team at my side, but grabbing somebody's garbage was pretty simple stuff.

What was more difficult was to determine if it had been poisoned or not. I didn't have the expertise to analyze the icing myself, and I couldn't very well ask a chemical lab to do it for me. It was important, though, to secure the evidence before it disappeared into a landfill.

"Secure the evidence" instead of "take her garbage"? Oh dear, I really was getting back into the lifestyle, wasn't I?

And I have to admit, it made me feel younger than I had in years.

But I couldn't go on that little mission until well after dark. I didn't know when Gretchen went to bed or if she would even be able to sleep that night, but I decided that if I went past around midnight, she certainly wouldn't be up and about, and neither would anybody else. The streets of Cheerville got quiet pretty early.

It was only a little past noon, so I had plenty of time to do some more sleuthing. Returning home to stow my pistol and rest my aching wrists, I gave Charles a call.

"How are you doing?" I asked after he picked up.

"Oh, not so good, I'm afraid. Yesterday left me exhausted. There were all the forms to fill out and officials to talk to, and I stayed up late with Gretchen last night. It was a most trying day. In fact, I'm at home. Oscar is taking care of things at the funeral parlor."

Oscar was his son, a quiet man whom I didn't know well. He was set to inherit the family business, or at least what was left of it.

I found it interesting that Charles had stayed with Gretchen after the officials had all left. Until late into the night, no less. I remembered that reassuring hand stroking her back.

"So what did the county coroner say? Was it a heart attack like we suspected?" I asked.

"Oh, he hasn't had time to see Lucien yet. He doesn't work on Sundays, and Mondays are always busy for him. Plus, there was a traffic fatality on the highway late Saturday night, and he has to take blood samples to check if the man had been drinking. The fellow swerved into another vehicle and injured the occupants, and the insurance company wants to know if he had been drinking."

"Oh. So when will he get to Lucien?"

There was a pause.

"I don't know. Is there some sort of rush?"

I bit my lip. I'd pushed him too hard.

"No," I said with a sigh. "I guess I just wanted some closure. It's hard when it's someone you know."

Charles's next words came out sympathetic. "Yes, yes it is, Barbara. It's got me thinking about my poor Laura. Everybody thinks morticians get used to this sort of thing, but we don't. Every customer who comes through my door tugs at my heart a little. Especially the young ones like that fellow who died on the highway. His family wants an open-casket funeral. The coroner let me take a look at him, and it's going to be a heck of a job to make him presentable."

"I see."

"But to answer your question, I suppose the coroner will get to Lucien this afternoon or tomorrow morning."

I made some quick calculations. The coroner would almost certainly notice the symptoms of poisoning. As far as I knew, those didn't disappear when rigor mortis set in. He'd take a blood test, send it off to the lab, and probably tell the police before the results came in. That meant the police would start sniffing around tonight at the very earliest, or more likely, tomorrow or even the next day.

It was impossible to tell for certain. All I knew was that I had to get that evidence before it disappeared. If the police came and asked Gretchen some initial questions, she'd get scared and get rid of the garbage. Which meant I had to snatch it before they arrived.

Which meant I had to go in broad daylight when

there were people out and about in the neighborhood.

I felt a little tingle of adrenaline at the thought that I'd have to take a risk. My my, I really was enjoying this a little too much, wasn't I?

Better now than later. If I had to do it in the daytime, it should be before people got off work and school. I only had to hope that Gretchen still had her garage door open and her blinds down.

She did. I made a slow pass by her house and saw no sign of her. Her car was still in the garage, so unfortunately, that meant she was home. Luckily, the garage door remained open. It was that kind of neighborhood. Nobody expected a burglary, let alone a murder.

I parked my car a bit down the street and out of sight of the house and then strolled in plain view along the sidewalk, keeping an eye on Gretchen's windows. If she looked out, I could simply walk up to her front door and ring the bell, saying I wanted to check in on her again. That looked suspicious but not damning.

I kept my eyes focused on those windows as I approached. None of the curtains twitched. Taking a deep breath, I casually walked into the garage, cutting across the neighbor's lawn so my shoes didn't crunch on the gravel driveway.

Now came the tricky part. I tiptoed to the door to the laundry room and pressed my ear against it. I couldn't hear a thing. Gretchen was either sitting alone mourning her loss or checking on plane tickets. Whatever she was doing, she wasn't being noisy about it.

As quietly as I could, I opened the bin and pulled out the garbage bag. I had to bank on the chance that she wouldn't open the bin again before she took it to the curb. The bag being so light compared to the bin, I doubted she would notice it had been removed as long as she didn't look inside.

If she did notice the bag had been removed, she'd be alerted to the fact that someone was onto her, assuming she was the murderer. If she wasn't the murderer, she'd only be thoroughly confused.

I peeked out the garage door. The blinds remained down, and no one was in sight on the sidewalk.

With as relaxed an air as I could muster, I cut across the neighbor's lawn again and headed for the sidewalk, angling away from Gretchen's house.

Just then, her neighbor opened his front door.

He was a younger man, in his early thirties, wearing a business suit and a preoccupied look. He made a beeline for the Lexus parked on the curb. He looked like a businessman who had come home to have lunch with his wife and now needed to hurry back to work.

He barely glanced at me even though I was on his lawn carrying a garbage bag.

"Good day. Lovely weather we're having!" I said in a chirpy voice.

"Hm," he nodded, checking his watch. Was this what Martin would grow up to be?

He didn't give me a second look as I got on the sidewalk and passed him. Nobody notices old people. I had always hated that. Now I saw that it had its advantages.

My hands shook with the best adrenaline rush I'd felt in years, and I nearly fumbled my keys as I got into the car.

I took a deep breath.

"Mission accomplished," I reassured myself.

Just as I pulled away, I saw Gretchen's curtain pull back and her face appear at the window.

She looked right at me.

# SEVEN

Frederick hurried out of the house as soon as I arrived, with that eager look that showed he had a prize client. After a quick thank-you, he was gone. He didn't even notice the tension that must have been clearly visible on my face. Gretchen had seen me on her street. She knew that I had shown up but didn't knock on her door. Should I call her and make some sort of excuse, like I had wanted to visit and decided not to at the last minute for fear that she was sleeping? That didn't ring true, because if that were the case, why would I call at all?

No, I'd been caught good and proper. If she was the murderer, the first thing she'd do was to check that bin. She'd be coming for me.

I had to avoid her now and hope she wasn't the murderer after all.

Shaking my head at my own ill fortune, I entered my son's home. At least Gretchen didn't know where Frederick and his family lived.

Martin was playing *Call of Duty* on the Xbox as usual, his feet, encased in dirty socks, propped up on the coffee table.

"Hi, Martin!" I said, sitting down beside him.

I got a grunt in return, almost drowned out by the sound of a bunker exploding. Just a big boom, and that's it. No falling concrete or secondary explosions from the enemy's ammunition or anything. They really needed to work on their sound effects.

"How was school?" I asked, forgetting myself and stroking his hair.

"Stop!" he said, yanking his head away. "Fine."

"What did you study?"

"Stuff."

I sighed. It looked like that one glimmer of sympathy from the previous night was the only attention I was going to get.

I headed to the kitchen to make a phone call. If spending time with my grandson was going to be time wasted, I had a murder investigation to deal with.

I still needed to talk to Pauline, who was a prime suspect because she had been a jilted suitor. Being a senior citizen using a walker hadn't stopped her from affairs of the heart, so it might not stop her from a crime of passion.

As I tried to figure out just how to approach my conversation with her, a more obvious problem still bothered me—just how would a homebody senior citizen in a dull town know where to get a fast-acting poison and know how to use it? This wasn't exactly common information, and while we lived in the so-called information age, how would one of my reading group sift through all the junk sites on the Internet to discover how to really administer a poison and which one to use? Assuming they could get over that hurdle, how would they get their hands on the poison? The kind of poison that had killed Lucien wasn't your garden-variety toxin. It was a deadly poison that one would not normally be able to find.

The poison problem reshuffled my list of suspects. Charles was the only one who had knowledge of chemistry. Undertakers knew about all sorts of noxious substances used to pickle people. It wasn't much of a stretch to imagine him acquiring the knowledge of how to turn those people into corpses in the first place.

Besides him, Evon was the most educated of our group. In fact, she was the only woman in the group who hadn't been a homemaker. She'd been a school-teacher all of her adult life until she had retired a few years ago. She'd been a middle school teacher, however, teaching social studies while dodging spit-balls. That didn't make her a prime candidate as a poison expert.

Evon did, however, know how to use the Inter-net, having worked in schools long enough that it had become universal before she left. That meant she had the skills to look these things up.

The younger generation doesn't realize, or doesn't care, just how computer illiterate many people over sixty really are. Pearl proudly proclaimed that she had never been on a computer in her life and never would. I had to personally help Gretchen find recipes on the Internet because she couldn't get the hang of using a search engine. Pauline expressed a similar ignorance. Even Charles had mentioned that he left "that computer stuff" to his son.

I used my cell phone to call Pauline, closing the kitchen door so I didn't have to hear World War III in the living room.

She took some time to pick up. The voice that said hello was heavy with grief and fatigue.

"Hello, Pauline. This is Barbara. How are you doing?"

Stupid question, I know. But what else do you ask in this situation? "Hello, Pauline, are you sad because your jilted love died, or because you killed him and can't handle the enormity of your actions?"

Doesn't quite have the same panache.

"Oh, as well as can be expected," Pauline replied. "I just can't believe he's gone. He was such a fine man."

I decided to lead her on a bit.

"Yes, handsome too."

"Oh, so handsome! He was the last ray of sunshine in my twilight hours."

I rolled my eyes in a fashion that would have made Martin proud. She was talking like the character from *Endless Beach*.

"You know I loved him, don't you, Barbara?" she said, her voice cracking.

"Yes, I heard."

"I know it was wrong, but I couldn't help it. He made me crazy every time I saw him. He never acted as anything other than a complete gentleman, never led me on or anything like that, but his mere presence set me on fire."

I rolled my eyes again. This was getting pretty interesting, though. She seemed to have no intention of stopping, so I let her continue.

"It was like he turned me into another person. I felt crazy around him. I would have never opened up my heart to any other man the way I did with Lucien. He had that effect on women. He renewed them, just like Marcella after she found a new lease on life in that wonderful novel we read."

I resisted the urge to roll my eyes again. All of this eye rolling was making me dizzy. No wonder Martin sat on the couch all the time. With his amount of eye rolling, he'd fall over for sure if he wasn't comfortably seated.

Something she'd said stuck out in my mind.

"So he had this effect on other women too?" I asked.

"Didn't he make your heart race like a thoroughbred mare?"

I blushed a bit at the comparison.

"Well, he was nice looking, but no, I wasn't in love with him."

"Oh," she said, sounding surprised.

"Other women loved him too?"

"I know someone who loved him as much as I did, perhaps more."

"Really? Who's that?"

"Oh, that was said in confidence. Besides, it doesn't matter now. Nothing matters now."

"Perhaps we should console her."

"I'm sure she's inconsolable. Now I really must go, Barbara. Thank you for calling, but I'm exhausted. Shattered. I don't think we'll ever be the same again. I loved him. We loved him," she said, her voice coming out as a hoarse whisper.

She hung up. I stared at the phone, wondering about Pauline's words.

Who was this "we"? Someone else in the readers' group? I'm sure everyone, even Pearl, had noticed Lucien's good looks—pretty much the entire female population of Cheerville over fifty had—but "love" was an awfully strong word, especially coming from a woman who had been jilted by her own spouse and who had developed an attachment to another woman's husband.

So perhaps love was the motivation, just as I suspected. Perhaps this other suitor couldn't handle rejection as well as Pauline had? Or perhaps Gretchen, feeling beset on all sides by competition, had killed her husband in a fit of jealousy? Maybe even Pauline did it, angry that this other woman had succeeded where she had failed? I needed to learn more.

Frustrated, I put away my phone and turned to go back to the living room. As I opened the kitchen door I heard a strange sound—silence. Curious, I entered the living room.

What I saw there nearly gave me a heart attack.

The television was off. The Xbox was stowed away, and my screen zombie grandson was reading a book!

Could this be the same boy?

Then I noticed his feet propped up on the coffee table. Yes, it was the same boy.

"Hi, Martin!"

Silence.

"Martin, say hello to your grandmother," I said, imitating Frederick's mantra.

"Hi, Grandma," he mumbled, focused as much on the page as he usually was on the screen. Being ignored while he was reading somehow didn't hurt so much.

"What's that you're reading?" I asked.

Martin moved the cover so I could see it and kept on reading.

*Dragon's Fire Book Five: Dragon's Bane.*

A colorful cover showed a dragon flying through the air and breathing flames that spelled out the title. Below stood three young teenagers—a boy and a girl in armor and wielding swords flanking a boy in robes with hands glowing like he was casting a spell. I was impressed that the girl got to be a warrior. Most of the girls in these books had to be the spellcaster since a warrior was a "tough guy" role. I did notice that she was bigger chested than any girl Martin's age had a right to be. Ah well, marketing.

"Is that good?"

Martin's eyes widened. "It's awesome!"

I wondered if there were any interior illustrations of the girl warrior.

An idea came into my head, not about the murder but about something almost equally important.

"Do you have book one?"

"Yeah."

"Can I borrow it?"

Martin gave me a curious look.

"Um, okay. Why?"

"I want to read it."

He stared at me.

"I don't think you'll like it."

"Well, I'd like to give it a try."

"Um, it's in my room somewhere. Don't move my stuff," he said, going back to his book.

A tremor went through my heart. Once while serving in the Northwest Frontier Province of Pakistan, a territory full of terrorists, warring tribes, and bandits, I'd discovered I had walked into a minefield. I had discovered this because I came across a skeleton. Well, actually, half a skeleton. The other half of the skeleton lay several feet away. Between the two halves of the skeleton was a shallow pit from where the mine had exploded, ripping the poor fellow in half and flinging his two parts into the air like an overeager toaster.

Walking out of that minefield had been only slightly scarier than the prospect of walking into Martin's room.

Have I mentioned that Frederick is one of those parents who thinks teaching his child independence means not taking any responsibility for his child's room? His wife, Alicia, is the same. They never clean up after him. As far as I know, they don't even go in there. They leave a stack of his clean laundry at his doorway and take whatever dirty clothes he dumps in the hallway to the washing machine.

I approached the doorway of Martin's room with more fear and trepidation than I had the kitchen in

Gretchen and Lucien's house. Dead bodies I can handle. They won't hurt me. Martin's room, on the other hand...

I stopped at the doorway with a gasp. It was worse than I'd imagined. Worse than Iraq in the nineties. Worse than Beirut in the eighties. Worse even than the South Bronx in the seventies.

Not a trace of carpet was visible, having been completely devoured by a wall-to-wall monster made up by discarded clothing, plastic weapons components, half-built Lego kits, cardboard boxes, empty wrappers, action figures, random bits of paper, and at least one dirty plate.

There were no straight angles in Martin's room, the corners and edges all softened by snowdrifts of T-shirts, miniature landfills of cereal boxes, bastions of football gear.

The place was a cocoon of crud. A nest of nastiness. A despond of detritus.

How the heck was I going to find a book in here?

The bookshelves were obviously the last place to look. There were no books on them—a lacrosse stick, a couple of empty soda cans, a hockey mask, and three dirty socks, yes—but no books.

I took a tentative step inside and nearly turned my ankle on a chunk of Lego. Adjusting my balance,

I decided on a safer tactic: I started sweeping my foot back and forth to move the mess in the hope of turning up the book.

Five minutes of work rewarded me with some visions that will haunt my dreams forever and *Dragon's Fire Book Four: Dragon's Hoard*.

Close, but no cigar. I put the book on the bookshelf and looked at Martin's hoard of junk. Certainly not as rich as a dragon's hoard, but perhaps bigger.

I went back to sweeping with my feet.

"WHAT ARE YOU DOING??!!" wailed an adolescent voice from the doorway.

Martin stood there, looking scandalized.

"I'm trying to find that book you're going to lend me."

"Why are you making a mess of everything?"

"Make a mess? Are you jok—"

"How can I find anything if you mess everything up?" Martin stomped into the room, expertly avoiding the landmines of toys and plastic pistols. He went to a heap of trash in the corner I hadn't excavated yet, stuck his hand in to the elbow, and pulled out *Dragon's Fire Book One: Dragon's Quest*.

"Well, I'll be a monkey's uncle," I whispered.

Martin looked at me. "Wouldn't you be a monkey's aunt?"

"It's just an expression."

He handed me the book.

"Are you really going to read it?"

"Yes."

"Why?"

"Well, if it gets you off the Xbox, it must be good, right?"

He gave me a teenaged eye roll and went back to the living room, where he buried himself in his book again.

I followed him and took a look at the cover. The same three kids were featured on the cover, although they looked slightly younger. A sticker on the cover said, "Reading is the only cool way to get high! Cheerville School District."

"What's this sticker?"

"Huh?"

"The sticker on the cover of this book. Why is reading the only cool way to get high?"

"It's a drug-prevention thing the school does," Martin said without looking up. "They gave me a free book."

"For what? Not selling drugs?"

Another teenage eye roll.

"No, for getting good grades in English."

For all his video game playing and incoherent

mumbling, Martin actually did get good grades.

"Shouldn't they give free books to kids who *aren't* doing well in English?"

Martin shrugged. "Good point. It's so you learn that there are better things than taking drugs and getting drunk and stuff."

"Well, I hope you don't get into any of that."

"And be a loser like Eddie? When I'm eighteen, I'm getting out of this boring town."

"Who's Eddie?"

"A guy in senior year. Pretty dumb. Got held back a year. He was dealing and got busted. His dad got him out because he was a minor then, but the school expelled him, and now he's stuck running his dad's pet store. He's a loser."

"Well, he's a good example of how not to live your life," I said as I put the book in my purse. I intended to read it. I wanted to connect with my grandchild, and I certainly wasn't going to do that with the Xbox.

As I zipped up my purse it hit me. For a full half minute I stood stock still, staring at nothing.

Eddie. A former drug dealer working at a pet store. If anyone could get access to illegal or dangerous substances, it was him. He had the knowledge, the dishonesty, and through his work, access to a wide range of chemicals. And at least two of my suspects had gone to the store where he worked.

I hurried over to the couch and gave Martin a big hug, followed quickly by kisses on his cheek and forehead.

"Eeew! Stop!"

The boy struggled. I didn't care.

"You are the most brilliant, most wonderful boy in the world! Thank you so much!"

"What are you talking about? You can thank me by getting off me!"

"No," I said, planting another kiss on his grimacing face. "I call grandma's privilege. You are a genius, my lovely little boy, and you don't even know it."

## EIGHT

"You shouldn't read in the car," I told Martin. "You'll get carsick."

"I don't get carsick," he said, his face still buried in *Dragon's Fire Book Five: Dragon's Bane.*

I didn't reply. Who was I to argue? The child was reading.

We were on our way to the Cheerville Pet Shoppe. Martin didn't want to go, but I had bribed him with the promise of dinner at his favorite hamburger joint. When he had questioned why I wanted to go, I said I was interested in buying a kitten.

Actually, I really was interested in buying a kitten. As much as I feared becoming one of those crazy old ladies with a dozen cats and a stinking house, I had to admit that in the evenings, once I had said good-bye to my few friends or left from having a nice dinner at my son's house, a deep loneliness came over me. It wasn't just losing James; it was losing my career, my place in the world.

I had sensed that this was coming and resisted retiring as long as I could, but government regulations finally came into play, and I was forced out on the basis of my age. Oh sure, they had given me a great send-off party, a severance bonus, and a splendid retirement package, but that didn't compensate for the change from operative to grandmother.

It was only after retiring that I realized just how huge a part of my life my job had been. You aren't a CIA agent from nine to five Mondays through Fridays. The job encompasses you. You're constantly reading reports or tailing targets or infiltrating nasty nations. I had loved every minute of it. Well, maybe not the intestinal parasites I'd picked up in Somalia, but most of it, anyway.

Now I would come home to my silent little house in my sleepy New England neighborhood, and the closest thing I could find for excitement was a romance novel or a spy movie on television. Even a kitten would be a welcome diversion.

So here we were, driving to a pet store to spy on a teenaged drug dealer while looking to buy a kitten.

I had no doubt Eddie was still dealing. A stint in juvenile hall rarely cured such cases. It had probably only made him more careful.

One might think that bringing a thirteen-year-old boy on such a mission was irresponsible, and I have to admit that's correct, but I couldn't leave him alone, and I didn't have much time to crack this case. Besides, we wouldn't do much snooping, just a preliminary reconnaissance. A little old lady with a bored grandson was just about the best cover you could have in such a place.

The shop was a big one for such a small town. Cheerville had an older-than-average population and, apparently, had more than its fair share of crazy cat ladies.

Crazier than that, as I was soon to discover.

When we entered, my ears were filled with the usual barking, meowing, and chirping you'd expect in a pet store, and my nostrils were filled with that musty scent that no amount of cleaning could banish.

Martin and I stood at the doorway and looked around. A row of cages held puppies and kittens, and suspended from the ceiling were numerous birdcages containing everything from budgies to Amazonian parrots. I spotted several rare species I hadn't seen since hunkering down in the jungles of Central America.

The birds were the least exotic of the lot. To one side stood several terrariums with snakes, spiders, and various giant insects. A doorway beyond them led to another room filled with aquariums filled with colorful fish. Next to the front door were the cash register and counter.

And Eddie. Martin didn't even need to point out Eddie. I knew him right away.

He looked about nineteen and sported a nose piercing and two big hoops through his earlobes. Not earrings, which I had long since learned to accept on men, but those discs kids are putting in their ears now to make giant holes in their earlobes. They looked ridiculous. Maybe that's why Eddie radiated a bad attitude.

Now, don't think that I judged him by his piercings and the tattoos I could see poking out from under his shirt. I had learned not to judge from appearances. You don't judge someone by the clothes they wear or the flags they wave or even the weapons they're packing but by their eyes.

And Eddie's eyes, frankly, scared me.

They were hard, with a confidence beyond arrogance and the flat, predatory look of a reptile.

I'd seen those eyes before—on drug barons, terrorists, career violent criminals—and they always meant trouble.

Those eyes passed over us with barely a glance. We were beneath his notice. I almost let out a sigh of relief that he didn't recognize Martin. I suppose thirteen-year-olds were just as invisible to nineteen-year-olds as seventy-year-olds were.

The next thing I noticed was the small crowd of young men and women lounging about with him. They looked as if they were in high school and a little older, all sporting defiant fashions of one kind or another. I couldn't keep track of the latest trends, and it didn't matter. I'm old enough to remember the beatniks, and then the hippies, the punks, the metalheads, the ravers, the grunge kids, and whatever it was these days. The looks changed, but it was all the same. The look always said, "I don't care what my parents and society think."

Actually, they cared what their parents and society thought more than most kids, which was why they were so obsessed with defying them.

A quick scan of their eyes revealed no murderous reptiles among them, just a Visine salesman's dream come true. All of these kids were high.

In a pet store.

Since when had that become trendy?

So, if these were Eddie's customers and not fellow gang members, I didn't have to worry about them much. I wondered if Eddie even had a gang or operated alone. I hoped for the latter, because I never liked being outnumbered.

Martin headed over to the kittens and peered in through the cages.

"What kind do you want, Grandma?"

"Um, I'm not sure," I replied, trying to focus on my purported reason for being here.

Normally, I find kittens distracting. They're cute and funny, and kitten memes are Facebook's only redeeming feature.

And these kittens were especially cute. Eddie might have been a dangerous drug dealer, but he did know how to take care of animals. The cages were spacious, and each held a couple of kittens, along with simple squeaky toys and rubber balls that the little darlings chased around. As we watched, one little tabby thwacked a rubber ball into the side of the cage, making it ricochet off the side and straight into the back of another cat's head.

The victim, a lovely animal of nearly pure white, blamed the tabby and leapt on him. The next moment, they were a rolling mass of fur until their fight knocked the rubber ball on a high arc and straight into their water dish. Both kittens got soaked and fled to opposite sides of the cage, staring wide-eyed at their invisible assailant.

We both laughed.

The cats weren't so cute that they distracted me from the trouble in the room. I noticed the kids were on the move. A few of them left, the bell on the door jangling. An important detail—I couldn't enter or leave the store without Eddie knowing. Some of the other kids went over to the terrariums.

We browsed the kittens for a while, and once we had overdosed on cuteness, I led Martin through the rest of the pet store. Eddie remained behind the counter, tapping away on the computer but really paying attention to everything going on in the shop. He had that slightly tense poise, that purposely turned-away face, that showed he wasn't actually focusing on the screen but rather on everything else.

I noted with interest that Martin avoided the terrariums. While any boy his age would be fasci-nated with snakes and spiders, he obviously didn't like the crowd over there. That reassured me. Much as I love Frederick and Alicia, they weren't giving Martin enough attention, and I feared he could go down the wrong path. It looked like he had some native common sense, though.

We went into the side room with the aquariums. It had dim blue lighting to highlight the under-the-sea theme. Seashells and netting and fake ship's anchors adorned the ceiling. A bit hokey, but the selection of fish more than made up for it. Giant tanks lined all four walls. Some held common fish like goldfish, while others held brilliant tropical fish with unreal colors.

Martin stopped to look at a navy-blue fish that looked a bit like a vertical pancake. Its tailfin was yellow, and it had two orange stripes along its body, as well as a white strip around its gills. Its lips were orange too, and it made little kissing motions as it swam lazily around the tank. The label told me it was a Scribbled angelfish. It didn't look much like an angel to me, but it definitely looked scribbled.

"Cool," Martin said. "You sure you don't want some fish?"

"There's a big aquarium in the city. You want to go sometime?" I asked, hoping for a field trip with my grandson. Anything to get him away from the Xbox.

My hopes were dashed the next moment.

"Nah, we went on a field trip there a couple of months ago."

We continued our circuit of the room, studying all the various fish. They were really quite remarkable. I had no idea that Cheerville had such a well-stocked pet store. It looked as if Eddie was good at something other than just selling drugs and looking menacing.

I paused in front of a small tank that contained only one mottled yellow-and-brown fish. The label said it was a pufferfish.

"Check this out, Martin," I said and tapped on the glass.

The fish immediately ballooned out to four times its original size and poked out spikes in all directions.

"Whoa! Cool."

"Can I help you?"

I jumped and spun around as fast as my old bones allowed me. Eddie stood right behind us.

No one sneaks up on me. No one.

But he had.

I put on my best little-old-lady face.

"Oh, we were just admiring all the lovely fish. What I'm really here for is one of those adorable kittens."

Eddie fixed me with a pair of eyes that really

belonged in one of the terrariums in the other room. He had a suspicious, predatory look.

"Shall I show you some?" he asked, his voice tense.

"Sure!" I chirped.

He led us to the other room. The front door jangled as the last of the stoner kids left. We were alone with him.

"This for you, little man?" Eddie asked Martin.

"No," my grandson mumbled, not looking at him.

"It's for me. I get so lonely at night, and I think a kitten would be the perfect thing."

"Weren't you in here earlier?" he asked, staring at me curiously.

"Um, no."

*You must have mistaken me for some other little old lady,* I thought. *I wonder which one?*

Eddie was wearing a loose, long-sleeved shirt and those baggy pants that kids liked to wear nowadays. It was the perfect ensemble for hiding a firearm. I didn't see any obvious bulges at the waistband or the tops of his boots, but that didn't mean he didn't have a gun hidden there. If he could sneak up on me, he could hide a gun from me. My own firearm was back home.

Martin stared at the kittens, edging a little away from Eddie.

"How about that one?" he asked, pointing at a little yellow guy.

"Sure, let's take him."

"Oh, wait, maybe that one," Martin said, changing his mind.

"Sure, that's fine." I wanted to get out of there.

But Martin couldn't make up his mind. He forgot his nervousness around Eddie as he played with all the kittens. After what seemed like forever, he finally settled on a lovely little tortoiseshell. With a profound sense of relief, I bought the cat and a carrying case and paid in cash. I didn't want to use a credit card and let Eddie discover my name.

At last we left the shop and got back out into the open air. I allowed myself to sigh in relief.

"Cool kitten, Grandma," Martin said, carrying the plastic case and grinning.

"What shall we call her?" I asked my grandson.

"How do you know it's a her?"

I smiled.

"Do you really want to learn the facts of life from your grandmother?"

Martin looked like he was about to have a seizure. I let him off the hook.

"Tortoiseshells are almost always female. Males are very rare, so rare that I'm sure the store would advertise the fact so they could charge extra."

"Oh. How about Dandelion?"

"That's an odd name for a cat of this color."

"It's the familiar in the *Dragon's Fire* books."

"Dandelion it is then."

"Mission accomplished," Martin said in his best *Call of Duty* voice. "Let's go get a burger."

I nodded. Yes, mission accomplished. Now I knew how Lucien had been poisoned.

# NINE

It's called tetrodotoxin, and it's deadlier than cyanide. It can cause death in a healthy adult within two hours, often as quickly as twenty minutes. Almost immediately after ingestion, the victim feels a tingling sensation in his lips and mouth, as well as his extremities. This is quickly followed by dizziness and vomiting. Lucien never got to the vomiting stage because the dizziness made him fall over and crack his head on the floor. That either caused a brain clot or, perhaps, a heart attack.

So the fall was what actually killed him, but it was the tetrodotoxin that made him fall in the first place.

And where does one get tetrodotoxin? In puffer-fish. That little guy we saw swimming around the fish tank in the Cheerville Pet Shoppe had enough tetrodotoxin to kill thirty people.

Pufferfish are famous for being a poisonous fish that's considered a delicacy in Japan, where it's called *fugu*. Chefs have to take a special course on pufferfish preparation before they are legally allowed to serve it, and even so, around a hundred people die from eating the fish every year, usually at hole-in-the-wall restaurants or from home cooking where the chef doesn't have a license and is breaking the law.

I've never understood why people risk their lives to eat fugu, but perhaps I'm just not a gourmand. James and I tried it once in Tokyo. We didn't want to, but the yakuza we had to make an arms deal with insisted. We were unimpressed. The sushi was a bit rubbery and had little flavor at all. The fried fugu that came later was tasty, but so was everything else on the menu, so why bother?

The next table had told us why. It was full of drunk businessmen eating fugu and speaking to each other in loud, boastful tones. This wasn't a food to eat for enjoyment; it was a food to eat for the bragging rights.

So I had my murder weapon. Someone, almost certainly Eddie, had killed a pufferfish and extracted the poison. This is a fairly basic process, and I was sure Eddie was up to the task. Contrary to popular belief, besides your low-level street dealers, most drug dealers are actually quite intelligent. They run a high-risk, high-profit business, and the stupid ones don't last long. Eddie, for example, kept a large pet store with a wide variety of animals well kept and well stocked. He was also clever enough to include lots of snakes and spiders to attract the kids so he could then sell them drugs. I wouldn't have been surprised if Eddie's self-trained knowledge in animals and chemicals was equivalent to bachelor's degrees in zoology and chemistry.

Another thing about successful drug dealers—they never sampled their wares, at least not on the job. Eddie had been quite sober when I saw him in the pet store.

That made him all the more dangerous.

I would have to be careful when I showed up at closing time and confronted him.

Yes, he was the key. If I could get him to confess, I'd have my murderer and I'd have my accomplice. Assuming I didn't make myself another victim.

The shop closed at eight. I'd already dropped off Martin, and it was now a quarter past seven. I was back home caring for Dandelion, who had taken to her new home as any kitten would—the instant I'd let her out of the box, she'd bolted under the couch and hadn't been seen since.

Ah well, I'd grow on her. At least she wasn't stuck in a cage being stared at by stoned kids anymore.

In the meantime, I had some preparations to make.

I removed my 9mm automatic pistol from its lockbox and checked it. I'd cleaned and oiled it right after visiting the shooting range, of course, but when you were entering a potential combat situation, it was best to double check everything. The last thing you needed was a jam at a critical moment.

Everything looked in top condition, and I made sure I had a full magazine. I placed it in my purse. Carrying it like that was illegal, but sometimes you had to break the law to uphold it. I knew Eddie was dealing drugs, and I felt ninety-nine percent sure that he had supplied the poison that had killed Lucien. Now all I had to do was prove it.

At gunpoint.

Just as I zipped up my purse, there was a knock at the door.

A cold prickling ran down my spine. Could Eddie have tailed me? That meant he knew where Martin lived, too.

I moved out of the line of sight of the door.

"Who is it?" I called, unzipping my purse and gripping the gun.

"Gretchen."

Okay, that wasn't as bad as I'd feared, but it was still plenty bad. I took a peek through the door's spy hole. She was alone, and she looked mighty cross. I put the purse strap over my shoulder and left the purse open so I could keep my gun near.

Taking a deep breath, I opened the door.

"Why were you at my house earlier?" she demanded before even stepping inside.

I had been expecting this question but had hoped to find the murderer before having to answer it. As it was, I didn't have a decent answer.

"I was worried about you, and so I came to visit, and then I decided to leave you alone at the last minute."

I prayed she hadn't noticed her garbage was missing.

"Why did you go in my garage?"

She stepped inside as she asked this. I did a quick check of her stance. Her hands were balled into fists, knuckles white in anger. If she was holding any sort of weapon, it would have to be a small one.

A vial of poison, perhaps?

Otherwise, I saw no physical threat from her. Despite her boasts of being healthy, I knew I could beat her in a fight unless she had an ace up her sleeve.

And I knew I had an ace up mine. Or in my purse, rather.

As my eyes did their work, my mind did its own. She had demanded to know why I had been in her garage, not why I had stolen her garbage. Either she was hiding the fact that she knew that, or she didn't know why I had entered her garage.

But if she knew I had stolen her garbage and didn't want me to know she knew, she wouldn't have mentioned the garage at all. She would want to lull me into a false sense of security and poison me when the opportunity arose.

I put on a contrite face.

"I'm sorry, Gretchen. I listened at the door. I didn't want the neighbors to see me snooping at the front door, so I went into the garage and listened there."

"You were spying on me?" Her voice came out shrill.

Taking a gamble, I said, "I was worried about knocking on your door, so I listened to hear if you had other company. Instead, I heard you crying. I wasn't sure if you wanted to be left alone or not, so I got cold feet and left."

"Nonsense! You were mooning over Lucien. Can't you people leave us in peace now that he's dead? I am so tired of women flirting with my husband. Oh, I expected it with some of these bored housewives, but I thought more of you. You had a career. But no, you're just like the rest of them. Lucien always tried to be patient with you silly old girls, and I did, too. And this is the thanks that I get?"

Gretchen blinked and focused on the floor behind me.

"I didn't know you had a cat."

Dandelion had chosen this moment to peek out from under the sofa. As soon as the kitten saw Gretchen notice her, she disappeared back beneath the furniture.

Gretchen's eyes roved around the room and noted the cat carrier by the door and the free brochure for new pet owners the Humane Society gave out with each purchase that sat on my coffee table.

"Oh, you just got it."

Then she turned and glared at me.

"Well, at least you'll have some company. You're certainly not welcome at my house ever again."

With that, she stormed out the door. Well, "stormed" is a rather grandiose term for walking slowly but angrily out of my house. That's the problem with spending most of your time with senior citizens. Everything takes longer, including the awkward moments. Especially the awkward moments.

My mind and emotions were in a whirl. I didn't know what to think of her visit or her reactions, but I was becoming more and more convinced that she wasn't the murderer. Whoever killed Lucien had acted in cold blood. Gretchen wasn't acting cold at all. Plus her comments about Lucien being a loyal husband despite years of temptation sounded like the truth.

As she left, I made excuses about having to see my son and drove out, too. Luckily, her house was in the opposite direction of the Cheerville Pet Shoppe, and so we soon parted. I watched her through my rearview mirror as she rounded a corner and disappeared from view.

Even though I was pressed for time, I made a slow circuit of my block and came back to my own house. She was nowhere to be seen. Good.

Then I made a beeline for the pet shop and made

it just in time to see Eddie turn the sign from Open to Closed.

Acting like a flustered and dotty old lady, I shuffled out of my car, waving my hand frantically over my head at him. He frowned and waited for me.

"We're closed," he called through the glass once I made it to the door.

"Oh, I'm ever so sorry, but I forgot to buy kitty litter. You do have kitty litter, don't you? I'm afraid my darling little kitty is making a mess all over my floor."

"Go to the supermarket."

"Oh, I could, but you know how crowded the supermarket is. It's ever so busy with people rushing here and there and me with my bad heart. Would it be possible to sell me some kitty litter? It will just take a moment, and you were so nice today with my grandson, and I wanted to reward the business by coming back here. You'll get a regular customer out of me!"

He studied me a moment and then did something I didn't like at all—he glanced either way up and down the street.

"All right."

He unlocked the door. Adjusting my purse, I walked in.

I kept a close eye on him and tried to stay near the window.

"It's at the back," he said, jabbing a thumb in that direction.

There was no way I was going out of sight of that window. I eased my purse down a little more.

"Oh, could you get it for me? I'm afraid I'm not as strong as I used to be."

Not as quick, either, as it turned out, because two things happened at almost exactly the same time. I had been anticipating them and was prepared to react, but my reaction time was far too slow.

First, he reached over and flicked off the lights, plunging the shop into darkness.

Second, he lashed out at me.

## TEN

What was meant to be a right jab straight into my lovely and still moderately unwrinkled face turned into a glancing blow to my shoulder as I ducked to one side.

Even so, it was enough to knock me back. I stumbled and would have fallen except that I hit a rack of doggie chew toys that stopped me from doing a head-cracking Lucien imitation. The chew toys acted as a cushion and let out a chorus of squeaks as they kept me on my feet.

"What are you doing here?" Eddie demanded.

I could see him in the dim light filtering through the window from the streetlights. Given that it was darker inside than on the sidewalk outside, no one would spot us. I didn't see anyone out there, anyway.

He took a step forward, all muscle and menace.

"I said—"

What he said next is not fit for repeating. Not that I blame him. Getting a pair of wonderfully manicured nails jabbed into your eyes isn't conducive to courtesy.

I reached into my purse for the gun, ducking a blind swing from the drug dealer.

Ignoring the twinge in my back from the sudden move, I pulled out the gun, flicked off the safety and...

...had the gun knocked out of my grip.

Eddie put a strong hand around my throat. He squeezed, just a little.

Just enough. I froze.

Eddie's face came close to mine, his eyes glittering in the streetlight coming in through the window.

"Who the hell are you?"

He released the grip on my throat just enough to let me breathe and speak.

Gulping down air, I replied, "A friend of the man you killed."

Eddie got a puzzled look on his face. "Which one?"

Oh, that was not what I wanted to hear. Nineteen years old and already asking that question? That's a bad sign.

"The one you killed with tetrodotoxin. The police have already been informed, and they're on their way."

A smug smile spread across Eddie's face. My eyes were beginning to adjust to the dim light, and I could see him better, not that that was a good thing.

"Nice try, lady. If you had called the cops, you wouldn't have risked coming over. And what's this about poisoning some dude? I gave that tetrodotoxin to some old bag to off herself."

What?

While that was a surprise, I was more concerned about him telling me this. It meant he planned to kill me once he had found out what I was doing there.

"She used it to murder her husband," I told him.

Eddie gave a little shrug like he didn't much care what it had been used for. Then his grip tightened slightly.

"You have a gun and you know how to fight. Just who the hell are you? You an ex-cop?"

"Ex-CIA."

Eddie laughed as if that was the most ridiculous thing he had ever heard. I like to make opponents laugh. Underestimating me puts them off their guard, and when people laugh, they tend to raise their heads and squint their eyes, distracting their vision.

Eddie did that, right on schedule.

Just in time for me to simultaneously knee him in the crotch and punch him in the Adam's apple.

Eddie doubled over, holding his not-so-manly parts and choking. Unfortunately, that maneuver gave me a head butt that knocked me back against the chew toys and set off another chorus of squeaks.

Stumbling out of the way of the groaning Eddie, I nearly fell before righting myself and peering around for my gun.

I spotted it on the floor several feet away. I sprinted for it.

Well, sprinted in my terms, meaning I made for it at a tolerably fast walk.

Not fast enough. I heard Eddie moving.

Glancing over my shoulder, I saw him crab-walking toward the cash register. His private parts were still smarting, and it made his gait quite amusing.

His goal was less amusing. He was almost certainly going for a gun.

Only one thought passed through my mind—could a seventy-year-old woman move faster than a nineteen-year-old man with a severe if sadly temporary handicap?

The answer was—a tie.

I ducked down, scooped up my gun, and turned just in time to see Eddie reach over the counter and pull out a revolver.

He was just leveling it at my head when I fired.

The gun flew out of his hand and smacked against the window, cracking it.

I smiled. Shooting a gun out of someone's hand was a great trick, one I didn't get to use often enough. Usually in a gunfight, you kill first and ask questions never, but I had a murder to solve.

Plus, I had done it on instinct. I didn't have time to put on my reading glasses in order to see my gun sights.

Readjusting my aim to focus on Eddie's frightened face, I paused a moment to let the new state of affairs make it through his shocked consciousness.

He cradled his hand. A trickle of blood glimmered in the streetlight.

"Whoops, it looks like I nicked you. I do apologize. I meant to just hit the gun. I'm not as good as I used to be. Old people are so useless and uncool, aren't we?"

"Why is the CIA hunting me?"

"Oh, you believe me now? We aren't hunting you. It's just that the poison you sold was used in a murder, the murder of someone I knew. So, who did you sell it to?"

Eddie sneered.

"I don't have to tell you anything. I got my rights."

I adjusted my aim and sent a bullet through the saggy part of his pants. The bullet cracked through the window and flew out into the street. A public safety hazard, I know, but also a good way to get the police to come.

"Some old lady, I don't know her name," he said, trembling and staring at the gaping hole in his pants. His hands were raised above his head now.

"You sure? Next time I'll aim a bit higher. I don't have my glasses on, but you're at point-blank range."

"Really, I don't know!"

"Describe her."

"Old."

"Yes, I got that. What else?"

"I don't know. They all look the same."

I aimed a bit higher.

"Um, she came in alone."

"Okay."

"She seemed to know what she was looking for."

"Go on."

"She knew I was a dealer and said that she wouldn't tell anyone that I was still in the business as long as I sold her the stuff. She knew all about tetrodotoxin."

"Now we're getting somewhere. What else did she buy?"

"Nothing."

"Not an aquarium or supplies or anything?"

"No."

"Had she ever been in the shop before?"

"Not that I can remember. Like I said, they all—"

"They all look the same, I know. Say that again, and I might just have to shoot you."

I cocked my head, thinking about what he had told me. This had taken an odd turn.

"Did she use a cane or a walker?"

"No, she walked fine. Not as healthy as you but pretty okay."

I furrowed my brow. That could only mean Gretchen or Evon. But Gretchen had come in to buy aquarium supplies with Lucien and Pauline. Perhaps Eddie simply didn't remember her.

But how did Gretchen or Evon know he was a dealer?

Then it struck me. Evon had been a school-teacher. Even though she had retired a few years before Eddie got thrown out of high school, she still attended those school board and PTA meetings. Plus, she socialized with other teachers, both retired and active. She would have heard all about him.

Evon.

Despite her hypochondria, she was one of the healthiest and most active of our group. She still drove by herself and knew how to use computers. She could have easily researched tetrodotoxin and learned how to find it and administer it. Now that I recall, Evon had once gone into the kitchen to help Lucien clean up, and he had told her that he could do it himself. That must have been when she'd caught him scarfing that last piece of lemon cake. She would have guessed that he did this all the time, perhaps sneaking a peek into the kitchen on another occasion. She was always getting up to check on people's work as if she was still running a classroom.

I thought back to her actions at the last meeting of the Cheerville Active Readers' Society. She had been fluttering around like a butterfly as usual, reaching over the table to show people their places in the book, especially Pearl, who was a bit slow. I hadn't really noticed her behavior because that was how she always acted. Looking back, I could see that it had given her plenty of opportunity to spike that last piece of cake.

Once Lucien had fallen over dead, she had stayed in the living room with Pearl instead of heading to the kitchen. That must have been to hide her guilty expression. Presumably, this was her first murder, and she didn't want to expose herself with any inappropriate reactions. Also, on some level, she knew she was a hypochondriac and must have been aware that facing death she had administered might cause some sort of breakdown.

Perhaps she also feared coming into any more contact with the poison. That was probably at the root of her "dying" right after the murder. Handling the poison, however carefully, must have made her worry that she had poisoned herself. She had probably agonized for hours over whether to call me or not. Calling a real doctor had been out of the question because they might have detected what kind of poison it was and incriminated her.

But why kill Lucien at all? How could someone

who feared invisible germs so much that she ran through gallons of disinfectant every month summon the courage to handle a deadly poison and sprinkle it on a cake that would have to sit in front of her for at least several minutes? She must have had an enormous amount of motivation to overcome her fear.

But what motivation?

Eddie was still staring at me, waiting for my next move. I cocked my ear, hoping to hear the approaching wail of a police siren. I heard nothing.

Then I realized that, since our little gunfight, less than a minute had elapsed. Time stretches out in situations like these.

"Move over there," I said, indicating the aisle.

Once he had stepped well away from his gun and my purse, I edged over to them.

I was about to flick on the light in order to see better and also to advertise the fact that there was trouble inside the shop, and then I thought better of it. Anonymity has its benefits. I didn't want the gossipmongers of Cheerville wagging their tongues about how that newcomer Barbara Gold was seen holding a gun on a drug dealer. Anonymity had gotten me to the verge of cracking this case. Better if everyone thought I was a sweet, harmless little old lady.

First I picked up Eddie's gun, hissing as my back twinged again. Eddie took that hissing as a threat and raised his hands higher above his head.

Fine by me. Another twinge, another hiss, and I got my purse.

Placing Eddie's gun inside, I was startled when at the same moment my phone rang.

It was Gretchen.

"Hello, Barbara. I wanted to apologize for my behavior earlier. I shouldn't have snapped at you like that. I came across as downright menacing and suspicious."

At the time, she certainly had, but in retrospect, it had only been the overreaction of a grieved widow. I knew that now.

"That's all right, Gretchen, considering the circumstances."

"So what are you doing at the moment?"

"Oh, nothing important," I said, grinning at Eddie.

"Yes, well, the truth is I don't want to be alone right now. Evon has kindly offered to come over, and I'd like you to come over, too."

"What? Is she there yet?"

"No, but—"

"Don't let her in. I'm coming right over! I'll explain later."

I glanced at Eddie. What to do with him? Even if someone was on the phone to 9-1-1 right now reporting the shots, the police wouldn't arrive for at least another couple of minutes, plenty of time for him to get away. They'd track him down, of course, but who knew how much havoc he'd cause in the meantime? I couldn't risk bringing him along in the car, and stuffing him in the trunk would take up too much time, plus if the police came while I was doing that, I would have too much explaining to do.

So I chose the only practical solution—I shot him in the leg.

The drive over to Gretchen's house nearly got me killed twice—first when I ran Cheerville's only red light and came within inches from getting sideswiped by an SUV and the second time when I almost veered off the road making an anonymous call to the police saying I'd heard shots fired inside the Cheerville Pet Shoppe.

My heart turned to ice as I pulled up outside Gretchen's home. Evon's car was already parked outside.

Hobbling over to the door, back twinging from too many sudden bends, body hurting from several bruises that I had just now begun to notice now that the adrenaline had started to wear off, I frantically rang the bell.

I almost fainted with relief when Gretchen answered the door.

"Do you feel all right?" I demanded.

Gretchen slumped. "Of course not. I—"

"Any tingling in your extremities or mouth? Any saliva buildup?"

"Barbara, what on earth are you—"

"Have you eaten anything since Evon came over?"

I was almost hysterical now. I fought to control myself, realizing that I was making a scene. I always got a case of the nerves after a gunfight. During the fight, I always acted calm and cool, as one should. I've seen people who got a case of the nerves during gunfights. They generally ended up on the floor.

Evon's head poked around the corner. She stood in the living room and looked down the front hall at us.

"No, why?" Gretchen asked.

I pointed at Evon.

"Because that woman poisoned your husband."

"That's ridiculous!" Gretchen shouted, glaring at me. "How could you say—"

A shriek and a wail from the living room changed her opinion abruptly. I pushed past Gretchen and hobbled down the hallway. Gretchen followed.

Evon was slumped on the couch, sobbing. For a moment, we stood and stared at her in silence. I kept my hand close to the opening of my purse. I didn't think I would need my gun, but it paid to be prepared.

"You did poison him, didn't you?" I said at last. "You bought some tetrodotoxin from Eddie at the pet store, and you put it on the last piece of lemon cake, knowing Lucien would eat it. You knew Eddie had been kicked out of school for dealing drugs, and one look at the crowd hanging around the pet store told you he was up to his old tricks. You wanted a fast-acting poison that was easy to administer and hide, and tetrodotoxin is one of the deadliest poisons in nature, and completely legal to purchase. All you need to do is buy a pufferfish."

Gretchen looked from me to Evon and back again. The look on her face showed she couldn't believe what she was hearing, but Evon wasn't denying anything.

Clarity dawned on Gretchen's face. "You loved him too, just like Pauline! I always suspected it."

Evon nodded.

"It's just as I thought," I said. "Pauline hinted that she wasn't the only one to be in love with your husband, Gretchen, and although she didn't name any names, who would confide that secret to her more than her best friend?"

"Pauline had nothing to do with this," Evon objected. "She would have never hurt him. That was the problem."

"What do you mean?" I asked. I still didn't quite understand why Evon would do such a thing.

She looked at me, eyes wide. I saw madness in those eyes.

"That man was like a disease, a disease that made women insane. Look how he made Pauline act. She never recovered from her husband leaving her for a younger woman, and then along came Lucien, all courtesy and good looks, and sent poor Pauline into a swoon. She knew it was mad; she knew she was setting herself up for disappointment, but she couldn't help herself. Instead of putting her unhappy years behind her, she ended up making her life worse. I was the same. I fell for him too. Everyone always wondered why I never got married. It's because I never found any man that was up to the mark. Then I found Lucien, and I knew I couldn't have him. That killed me inside."

"So you murdered my husband because he rejected you, like he rejected Pauline," Gretchen said, her face white with shock.

Evon shook her head. "He never rejected me because I never told him. I knew what his response would be. That man is a disease. Who knows how many other hearts he's broken."

"But he never led you on!" Gretchen shouted.

"He couldn't help it. I don't blame him. He was just a carrier, unaffected by the disease but giving it to everyone else. The only way to stop a disease is to get rid of the carrier."

"So you poisoned the cake," I said. "How?"

Evon gave a little shrug. "It was easy enough. Eddie concentrated the poison into a few drops of liquid and put it in a small vial, small enough that I could hide it in the palm of my hand. When I pointed out the page to you, I had the vial hidden in my palm, covered with three of my fingers. As you and everyone else looked down at the page, I withdrew my hand and poured it onto the cake. Then I tucked the vial into my pocket and threw it away later."

"How could you handle the poison without being terrified?" I asked.

"I *was* terrified. Tetrodotoxin isn't a contact poison; it has to be ingested, but I was so worried. I wiped my hands with a handkerchief that I later threw away. And I washed my hands what felt like a thousand times. I haven't eaten since I did it because I was afraid of touching any food that would go into my mouth. Even so, I felt sure for a time that I had poisoned myself too. That's why I called you."

"But you hadn't poisoned yourself," I said. "In fact, you're quite healthy. I'm afraid you're going to have to live with this for a long, long time."

"Oh, if the poison doesn't kill me, one of my other maladies will. I know I'm not long for this world, but at least I've made it safer for other women. I'm so sorry I had to do it this way, Gretchen, but I've saved you, too. Now you don't have to worry about people trying to steal your man. I'm so sorry."

Evon buried her face in her hands and started sobbing once more. Gretchen slumped in a chair, staring at her with a mixture of horror and disbelief.

I sighed. What a sad end to a life. While I understood now how lonely Evon had been, she had been a contribution to her community. She had taught for three decades, helping generations of children, and continued her work in education afterward. And all that time, her loneliness had fed her madness and led to this. She would be found guilty of first-degree murder. At her age, even the most lenient sentence a judge could give for such a crime would end up being a life sentence for her. Even worse, she'd probably be sent to a prison for the criminally insane. What a waste.

Feeling weary, I pulled out my phone and called the police.

## CHAPTER 11

Martin and I chomped down on hamburgers at his favorite fast food place. It was the second time this week that I had treated him, and he couldn't believe his good fortune. He'd earned it for helping me crack the case, not that I could tell him that. I didn't want him or anyone else knowing my secret.

Well, someone knew my secret now. After all this, it was bound to come out.

Cheerville Police Chief Arnold Grimal and I had had a long chat. I'd needed to speak with him about the details of the case and fess up to shooting Eddie. I have to say he took it well. There had been a tense moment when he said he'd have to tell the story to the press and there would have to be a court hearing concerning the Cheerville Pet Shoppe shooting. A call from the director of the CIA cleared all that up in about thirty seconds. Yes, I still have my connections there.

The police chief saw the light of day and promised to keep my past hidden from everyone else. Eddie was shot by an "unknown intruder" and thrown in jail for all the drugs they found in his car. Evon, sadly, was also in police custody and was sure to end her days behind bars. While Gretchen knew I had solved the case, she didn't know how or anything about my past. Being so wrapped up in her grief, she didn't much care.

So as far as Martin and everyone else were concerned, I was just a boring old grandmother.

Well, not so boring at the moment. We were talking about *Dragon's Fire Book One: Dragon's Quest*. While it didn't hold a candle to *Behind Open Curtains* (the characters were too young to ululate), it actually was fairly entertaining. And yes, there were internal illustrations, a disproportionate number of them of that warrior girl. Skara was her name, a skilled archer and swordswoman. Martin had a thing for her.

"Just wait until you read book two," he said, his

eyes eager above his bacon double cheeseburger. "There's some awesome fights in that one."

"I like that they all work together even though they're from different kingdoms that are fighting."

"Well, it's the adults who are making the wars. The three of them are too busy going on adventures and chasing dragons and stuff."

"Sounds much better than fighting a war."

"Unless you're fighting Nazis or terrorists."

"Or drug dealers."

"Sure. I have an Xbox game where you shoot drug dealers. You want to try it?"

"Um, I don't think that's really my thing," I replied, blushing. "Shooting drug dealers is something best left for the young."

"There aren't any drugs in the *Dragon's Fire* books, but there are zombies. Actually, sort of magically cursed people who aren't really dead so they aren't really zombies. Pretty cool, though. Skara has a big fight with them."

"I haven't come to the zombies yet."

"They're in book three. Are you really going to read the whole series?"

"Yes."

Martin grinned and stole some of my fries.

"Cool!"

I smiled and took another bite of my gloriously fattening burger. It looked like living in Cheerville wouldn't be so bad after all. I figured after things calmed down a bit, it would go back to its usual tranquil and dull routine, but I had kept my friendship with Gretchen, was thoroughly enjoying *Behind Open Curtains* and had already ordered the author's other novels, and had finally made a connection with my grandson. I guess with all that, I could handle a bit of dullness.

Assuming nobody else got murdered in Cheerville.

## ABOUT THE AUTHOR

Harper Lin is a *USA TODAY* bestselling author.

When she's not reading or writing mysteries, she loves going to yoga classes, hiking, and hanging out with her family and friends.

For a complete list of her books by series, visit her website.

www.HarperLin.com

.

Printed in Great Britain
by Amazon